THE TAURUS TRIP

AN INNER SANCTUM MYSTERY

by Thomas B. *Bouchard* Dewey, 1915-

SIMON AND SCHUSTER

New York

SECOND PRINTING

SBN 671-20699-0
Library of Congress Catalog Card Number: 72-130470
Designed by Irving Perkins
Manufactured in the United States of America
By The Book Press, Inc., Brattleboro, Vt.

THE TAURUS TRIP

1

MABEL DANDELO, seventy-one, died the other day, under mysterious circumstances, as the early paper put it. Actually the evidence of mystery was slight. It consisted of some blood on Miss Dandelo's head and face and the fact that she was found on the floor of her kitchen, with the door to the service porch ajar. The later editions explained that her position on the floor indicated she had been entering the kitchen from the service porch, which was why the door was open, and had fallen as the result of a heart attack, hitting her head on the stove, which was why there was blood on her head. There was some blood on the stove too.

She was an older woman, and everybody dies. But Mabel Dandelo was not just one of everybody. I knew her a little, not long, but long enough to learn to admire her. I did a job for her. Those of you who are forty or better, or worse, will remember her as Mary Dane, a silent screen star of the twenties. By the time I knew her the glory days were long gone. All that remained visible to an outsider were some pictorial mementos on the walls, a certain far-off look in Mabel Dandelo's fine blue eyes, and a daughter named Abigail Caccelli, who was as easy to look at as her mother must have been in 1926.

But Abby Caccelli fits in farther along. The first of the family to come to my attention was Mabel Mary Dane Dandelo, who lived in a concrete house in a canyon on Los Angeles' conglomerate west side. I began the drive to her place climbing from Sunset Boulevard, and finally reached the summit known as Mulholland Drive, started down toward the Valley and found the destination within a hundred yards.

The approach was startling, even unnerving. The massive concrete façade hung on the sheer cliffside of the canyon, and I was bearing down on it at forty miles an hour when I realized I would have to fly through the air for at least a hundred feet if I kept to the route. The road curved around the edge of the canyon; the curve was badly marked and I made it noisily, skidding on the outside wheels and leveling off barely in time to come to a stop at a closed wooden gate marked "Private—RING BELL."

The gate was of solid timbers and there was nothing to be seen beyond it from where I sat. I left the car, found a bell on a post to the right of the gate, and pushed it. I couldn't hear anything ring, so after a few seconds I pushed it again. At length I heard footsteps on the other side of the gate and I stepped back, moving fast when it began to swing open. Not till it stood fully open did I see the man behind the bell post, the guy who had activated the hinges.

He stood about six feet three, was somewhat stooped, lean and dark-skinned, completely bald, and would have applied for his social security a few years before. He wore

8

a pair of loose-legged slacks and a Hawaiian sport shirt, from the breast pocket of which protruded a pair of horn-rimmed glasses.

I told him I had an appointment with Miss Dane.

"Just drive in and park over there," he said. "Miss Dane is expecting you."

He had a low-pitched, deeply resonant voice, trained, an actor's voice.

There was a garage off to the right with blacktop parking space for two or three cars. The garage doors were closed. They were at some distance from the house, but the lot seemed small in proportion to the size and grandeur of the buildings. The place was well kept, the grass neatly clipped, the trees pruned and no excessive debris. Some of the trees were very old—eucalyptus, live oaks, magnolias, but there were several young fruit trees too, with irrigation basins around them.

The tall fellow had closed the gate, and when I got out of the car on the garage apron, he nodded toward the house, toward a side entrance set between a couple of potted cypresses. He walked that way with me, not crowding.

"Things look very good," I said.

"Thank you," he said, "we try to keep the place up."

He opened the door for me and, as if by afterthought, said, "My name is Peter Rinaldi."

"I'm Mac," I said, and we shook hands.

The name Peter Rinaldi rang a distant bell, but the

I thanked him and started the trip. The word "hall" had been used in an old-time sense. It was actually a ballroom in the great tradition—large black and white squares formed the floor; a crystal chandelier that must have weighed a ton was suspended from the ceiling; the floor itself was clear, and there were love seats and divans along three walls. In the fourth wall, on the front side, four high windows were draped with gold fabric. Outside, a broad porch with a waist-high stone railing formed a terrace and gave access to the main entrance. The knobs of the door were the size of young pumpkins and looked like pure gold, but I mistrusted that impression. The sound of my footsteps echoed behind me in the empty room.

The stairs descended at the far side of the hall and seemed cramped in comparison with the rest of the house. They were badly lighted and I used the banister going down. I couldn't see my destination because the steps right-angled toward the bottom. There was a vague fragrance of violets that grew stronger as I descended. When I made the turn at the lower landing, there was sudden light, lush, California light, and a California room —glass walls, casual, comfortable furniture set on many-colored rugs thrown over a base carpet. The windows looked out over a smaller version of the ground-floor porch, and beyond that into the canyon, beyond that to the ocean. A slender lady with soft yellow hair, dressed in old-fashioned lounging pajamas, sat in a Danish chair, looking at a magazine. The scent of violets became localized and specific. She looked up from the magazine, laid it on a table beside the chair and smiled.

"Hello, I'm Mabel Dandelo," she said. "Please sit down. May I get you something, a drink . . . ?"

"No, thank you," I said. "It's early."

"Perhaps later," she said.

I sat on a love seat, not quite directly facing her.

She looked out the high windows for a few seconds. The sunlight was good to her, especially to her hair. I couldn't tell whether it was all real or not, but it would certainly do until the real thing came along.

"I suppose you think," she said, "this is an awful lot of house for one little old lady."

"It's a great house," I said. "A privilege for me."

"It's very old," she said, "but it's well-made and we try to keep it up. It isn't always easy."

"I believe you."

"I'll tell you a secret—some of it I don't use. Some of the rooms are closed off."

"I shouldn't wonder."

"We used to give some good parties here," she said. "Even after my husband died, about three years ago, two or three parties. But no more. The party days are over. I'm no longer a hostess. I'm a professional guest."

"I would say you've earned the status," I said.

These polite rejoinders were all I could muster. I had no idea why I was there. I was just beginning to settle into a new Los Angeles office. The message from my answering service had said, "Please call for an appointment with Mabel Dandelo—" and there had been a number to call. When I called, Miss Dane herself had answered. "If you have the time, I'd like to consult with you on Thursday afternoon about four. I'd rather not discuss the matter by phone, if you don't mind." I had said, "Of course, Thursday at four." So I sat there in her sunlit living room, Thursday afternoon at about five minutes past four, and waited for her to discuss whatever the matter was.

"I was referred to you," Miss Dane said, "by an old friend, Fred Schiller."

Fred Schiller was a reporter on the Chicago *Tribune.* I had known him a long time. I hadn't known he had Hollywood connections.

"Old Fred," I said. "It was patriotic of him."

"He spoke very highly of you."

"Well, Fred and I have shared things from time to time."

"He was out here last week, on a vacation, and I asked him—he spent some time on the crime beat, you know. I don't know how that qualifies him as an authority on private detectives, but anyway I asked him. He said he thought you were in Los Angeles, and if I would put my best foot forward I might persuade you to listen to my problem."

Old Fred laid it on a little heavy, I decided. "Did you tell him about your problem?" I asked.

"Only in a very general way. Of course, I've only just met you, but so far, I would say Fred's judgment is sound."

"Thank you," I said. "I'll try to sustain the image."

I was getting a little impatient for her to come to the point. It was all very charming around there, but it occurred to my semicynical soul that silent screen stars are not always noted for affluence, and feminine charm, from time to time, has been exerted in this or that cause in lieu of cash. But it was a mean thought and I suppressed it for the time being.

"My problem, Mr. —" she said unexpectedly.

"Mac," I said.

"My problem, Mac, is hard to explain. There's so much I don't know."

"Maybe that's what I'm for," I said. "If you want to tell me what you do know . . ."

"Yes. You met Peter—Peter Rinaldi?"

12

"The man who takes care of things, yes," I said. "I was trying to place him."

"He's an actor, a very good one. He was in several pictures with me, and he stayed in the business after I retired—when I was married—and he did quite well for a time. But then things began to change in the industry and a lot of the old-timers had rough going— I'm sure you know all that. And Peter gradually became, well—permanently at liberty. He came to stay with us about six years ago. My husband was very fond of him, they used to play chess a great deal, and billiards. My husband wasn't in the industry in any way. He was an investment broker. It was good for him to have a man like Peter around. You see, we had only the one child, a daughter, and all our help was female and the place just seemed to be overrun by women, though naturally Joe never complained. But I could tell . . .

"Anyway, at first Peter was just a guest, but his pride wouldn't let him go on that way forever. He had a little money, very little, and it was only about two years ago he began getting his social security and a modest pension from the industry. He was, to be blunt about it, broke. So—he had always made himself useful around the place, he enjoyed working with the plants and trees, taking care of the lawn, that sort of thing, and he was handy at repairs and all, and it worked out that my husband persuaded him to stay on as a kind of houseman, with a regular wage and his own quarters in the house. I don't know how Joe managed it, but he could be persuasive when he set his mind to it, and he was really genuinely fond of Peter, and he found a way."

The light dimmed suddenly. I blinked and finally caught on that the sun had dropped out of sight over the far rim of the canyon. It had some effect on Miss Dane, too. She broke off her story and gazed out the window for about thirty seconds, some cloudy something about her face. I had the spooky premonition that her next words would be "After my husband died—"

"After my husband died," she said, and my fingers tightened on the arm of the love seat. "After Joe died, it was only natural that Peter should stay on. We were good friends. He was a tremendous help to me, and we were both too old to be concerned about gossip—there has never been any romantic thing between us, never was—and my daughter was about to be married and I didn't have any stomach for sitting in this house all by myself. So Peter stayed. I had enough income to continue to pay him. It was just a logical outcome."

I indulged in some private embarrassment over my reflections on charm and money.

Her voice changed, grew brisker, tighter. "That's the background," she said.

"I think I understand," I said. "Now a problem has come up."

"Yes. The problem is, Peter is leaving me. I don't mean that exactly. I mean he says he can't stay any longer."

"I see. Where would he go?"

"He says he's going to move to 'The Home,' as he calls it."

" 'The Home'?"

"For retired motion picture people. It's out in the Valley. It's a fine place and of course he would be welcome and well taken care of. No bother about pride and all that. He paid his dues."

I couldn't think of anything to say. I could imagine that Peter had just decided he had had enough of working around the house and—if there was a problem, so far it had only to do with Miss Dane's wish that he would stay with her rather than go away. I couldn't imagine anything I could do about that.

"I can see," I said, "it presents you with a problem, having to find somebody else . . ."

She shook her head impatiently. "No, it isn't that. That's not a problem. A nuisance maybe, but not a problem. It's that there's something strange going on, something funny about the whole thing."

"Oh?" I said.

"I think Peter's lying to me—I mean about why he wants to leave."

"What reason does he give?"

"Oh, something about . . . vague and mumbly, you know, about not being up to the work, not doing justice, earning his pay—the usual junk that men come up with."

Junk, sure, I thought, but it might be simply true in Peter's case. "What makes you think he's lying?" I said.

"Certain things that have happened recently. Number one: about a month ago, Peter went out one afternoon to go to the market, and he didn't come back for two days. Now that's all right by itself. He's free to come and go, it's not as if we were married, or as if I were helpless or anything. But it was mysterious. He called up from the market and said he was having the things sent out. He said something had come up and he would have to be away, possibly overnight. He would keep in touch with me. All right. That was all the explanation he gave me —something had come up.

"So he came back two days later, about the middle of the afternoon. He had a black eye and there were a

15

couple of bruises on his face. He was obviously unwell. I made him go to bed and stay there for the rest of the day and the night."

My response was automatic. "Does Peter drink?" I asked.

She shook her head, twice, very firm. "No," she said. "He can't. Constitutionally, he just can't. If he takes more than one drink, it puts him in the hospital—or used to. But when he got back after that two days, he wasn't sick in that way."

"He didn't discuss it with you at all?"

"Not a word, except that he had fallen in the dark and banged up his face. I didn't believe it then and I don't believe it now. But he never explained."

"All right. What happened next?"

"It was a couple of weeks ago. Two men came to the house to see Peter. He wasn't here—he had driven to Malibu to do some shopping; he thought he might do some fishing too. These two men came and I said Peter was out, and they asked if they could wait for him. I didn't like that too well and I explained that he might be a long time, but they were rather insistent, and they looked all right—respectable, well-dressed, you know—so I let them come in and wait, gave them a drink and so on. They waited about two hours and Peter didn't come. They finally left."

"They didn't identify themselves?"

"No."

"Did you ask them to identify themselves?"

"Well, no, I didn't. I ought to have, oughtn't I?"

"Yes. Did they talk between themselves at all while they waited?"

"Practically not at all. They made a few remarks about

the view, and the liquor—very polite—but then they didn't say anything at all. I didn't stay with them very long They . . . bugged me, as my daughter would say."

"They just sat here and waited for two hours and went away?"

"Yes. But they didn't go far. About half an hour after they left the house I saw them over there." She pointed toward the road outside, toward that dead man's curve I had managed to make approaching the house. There was a clear view of most of its length from where we sat. "Up on the road," she said. "Peter was there too, in his car. The two men had got out of their car and were standing in the road, talking to him. I saw Peter shake his head a couple of times, and finally the two of them got in their car and drove away and Peter came on home."

"Any explanation this time?"

"No. I told him about the two waiting for him and he just shrugged it off. He didn't say anything about meeting them on the road, so I didn't say I had seen them. That's all."

"Anything else happen?"

"Two days ago," she said, "Peter made his usual trip to the market—we have quite a long way to travel for supplies, by the way, and Peter usually does it by himself, because there are always extra little things, from the hardware store and so on, that I don't know anything about, and besides, he gets along better when I'm not tagging along, but he'll take me with him whenever I want to go, which isn't often. Anyway, he came in with a box of groceries and left them on the kitchen shelf for me to put away, which is my part of the job. And in one of the paper sacks, along with some onions, was a piece of torn envelope with a message written in pencil. The message read: 'Last chance Monday twenty-six-oh-five Redgrave before nine P.M.'"

"What did you do with the message?"

She picked up the magazine she had been looking at, riffled the pages and pulled out a piece of torn envelope.

"It's right here," she said. "I don't know what to do with it. I just kept it."

"You haven't mentioned it to Peter?"

"No. I didn't know how to handle it. After I found it, I called you."

I looked at it. The message she had quoted was scrawled in soft pencil across the paper. The part of the envelope that had been used bore a canceled stamp and postmark on one side and nothing on the other. Nothing was left of an address or return address. The postmark was illegible.

"What do you conclude from all this?" I asked.

She looked at me straight on with those blue eyes. "I think Peter's in trouble. I think that whatever the trouble is, that's what's making him go away. I don't think he intends to go to The Home at all. I think he's going away so this trouble—whatever it is—won't land on me."

"Have you asked him about it at all? About the trouble?" I said.

"Yes, last night. I said, while we were eating supper, 'Peter, are you in trouble?' And he just laughed. 'Me, in trouble?' he said. 'No, no trouble. The days of trouble are over.'"

"What did he mean by that?"

She shrugged. "Nothing—just a thing to say, like, 'I'm not in the movies anymore, how could I be in trouble?' It's like a joke."

18

"Why are you so sure the message in the onion sack wasn't meant for you?"

"Because—it's absolutely meaningless to me."

Reason enough. "Has Peter said anything about when he expects to leave?" I asked.

"Yes," she said. "Sunday, this coming Sunday."

I looked at the message again. "Last chance Monday—" I looked at Mary Dane and I looked out the window, where the canyon was turning dark.

"You've considered the possibility," I said, "that Peter just wants to get away, for a change?"

"Yes, I thought about that," she said, "but I don't think he does. Besides, those things I told you about, the bruises on his face, the two men, the message—I didn't just make them up."

"Of course. And your thought is that I may be able to find out what Peter's trouble is and . . . save him from it?"

"Something like that, I suppose. Just finding out would be worth something to me. If there is something we can do about it, so much the better."

"It may be some simple thing, some foolishness," I said, thinking aloud. "Or it could get into an extensive bit of research."

"I know. I'm prepared for that. I'll write you a check right now for whatever you need at this time."

"Well," I said, "basically I cost seventy-five dollars a day, plus extraordinary expenses. A hundred and fifty now will get me started. If I put in less than a day, there'll be a refund. A day is twenty-four hours."

She opened a drawer in the table, took out a checkbook and pen and started writing. Across the near canyon, a red

Jaguar made the death-defying circuit of the curve approaching the house. There was a girl at the wheel.

"One thing," I said. "Did you tell Peter you were calling a private detective? Does he know that's what I am?"

"No," she said. "I told him you were interested in writing a book about me, my movie career."

Do I look like a writer, I wondered, who has to write that kind of a book?

I got out my note pad and wrote down the address on the piece of envelope. I handed the envelope to Miss Dane as she handed me the check.

"I think you ought to give this to Peter," I said, "or leave it where he will find it."

"All right," she said, "I will."

"I'd better get started—unless there's something more you can tell me."

"I wish there was," she said.

"Have you mentioned any of this to anyone else, anyone at all?"

"Some of it, to my daughter, Abigail. She's an adopted daughter actually, but we're quite close, maybe closer than we might be otherwise. I told her Peter said he was leaving and that I thought maybe he was in trouble. I didn't tell her those details you know."

"Did you mention that you might call in a detective?"

"Yes . . . as I remember, I suggested that."

"Did she have any comment?"

"No. One reason we get along so well is that we don't make too many suggestions to each other. Live and let live."

"All right, I'll go now," I said.

I got up and she got up with me and gave me her hand, a cool, firm hand. She was a cool, firm lady. I liked her.

"You'll hear from me," I said, turning to the stairs.

"I hope so," she said. "Thank you for coming."

I climbed the stairs to the ballroom, where suddenly a movie was in progress. Swirling toward me over the giant checkerboard floor came a swinging, white leather miniskirt, a matching embroidered jacket, knee-high white boots and a crown of massed white curls. She was in a hurry. The boots slapped a tattoo on the parquet. Somewhere nearby, the cameras had to be rolling.

I stepped out of her direct path to give her flying room. She flew past me toward the stairs, looking straight ahead, and I went on toward the side door. It was hard not to stop and watch. I was still short of the door when she sang out, "Hey—!"

Given permission, I turned around and looked at her. She was poised at the top of the stairs, teetering a little in the high boots, her miniskirt still swinging around her longish, somewhat meaty legs.

"Yes?" I said.

"Are you driving down—that way?" she said.

"To Sunset, yes," I said.

"Can I ride with you? The damned Jaguar is busted."

"Certainly," I said.

"Just a minute," she said, starting down the stairs, "I have to see mother . . . wait for me . . ."

Her voice faded as she disappeared. She was better than her word. The white curls showed, rising from the stairwell, in less than a minute. She crossed the floor at a run. I barely managed to get the door open in time. Panting a little as she rushed through it, she said, "I'm Abigail Caccelli."

"My name is Mac," I said. "Car's right over there."

She beat me to it.

22

THE RED Jaguar was pulled up at an askew angle on the garage apron. There was no sign of Peter Rinaldi. I backed and turned and got onto the road while she adjusted her nylon thighs.

"Ouch!" she said. "It's hot!"

I could feel it through the padding of my trousers, stored sunshine. It would be stinging hot for her.

"You're saving my life, you know that," she said. "I have to be at the Beverly Hills Hotel in about fifteen minutes."

"We'll make it," I said. "What happened to the Jaguar?"

"Oh that mother! I don't know what happened. It stopped. I had to coast off the road . . . if the gate was closed . . . something else, man!"

I made it around that bad curve and we started down the canyon.

"You in the industry?" she said.

"Uh—no. I have my own business."

Her face brightened. "Oh, you're that detective guy, huh?"

"Yes. Yes, I am."

"Mother told me she was going to—what's it like?"

"What?"

"Being a detective, I mean, like James Bond?"

"Who's James Bond?"

"You know, Goldfinger and all that."

"James Bond was a writer," I said. "He created a character named Ian Fleming. No, it's not like that, ma'am."

"You're putting me on," she said.

"I guess so."

"Guess what I am."

"A lady detective."

She giggled. "An actress, silly. Don't I look like an actress?"

"Come to think of it," I said. "How is it going, the actress business?"

"Real good. I have to meet my director and some other guys at the Beverly Hills. I'm going to be a real star one of these days. They keep telling me—now I believe it. You have to believe it."

"I'm sure of that."

"If you don't believe it—you have to have self-confidence."

"Then by all means—"

"If you don't have self-confidence, it doesn't matter how much else you have. You're dead."

I made the turn onto Sunset and the traffic wasn't too bad going east toward Beverly Hills. It was pretty bad coming the other way. I thought we could make the hotel all right in time for her appointment.

"Peter's in trouble, huh?" she said.

"What do you think about it?"

"I don't know anything but what mother tells me—she

thinks he's in some kind of trouble. He's going to move out of the house."

"So I understand."

"Do you know what kind of trouble he's in?"

"No idea," I said. "I'll try to find out."

Her face went into a thinking posture. I could tell by the pursed lips and the half-closed eyes.

"I wouldn't want him to be in bad trouble," she said, "he's a good guy. He's been real good to mother. But if he really moves out, that could be a good thing."

"It could?"

"Yes. Then maybe mother would move out too. Get an apartment somewhere. That crazy house is no place for her, at her age."

"She seems to like it there," I said.

"She thinks she does. But if she had to be there all by herself . . . it bugs me. I hate to go there anymore."

"Well, we'll see," I said.

"If you could persuade her to move out . . ." she said.

"You're exaggerating my influence. I only met your mother today. I'm a minor employee."

"Well . . . anyway . . . what time is it?"

I looked at my watch and reported. "Four fifty-five," I said.

"Crazy," she said. "We'll make it."

"I think so."

She squirmed in the seat, frowned and slapped her thighs with both hands impatiently.

"Why is it," she said, "if you have an appointment, it always has to be like five o'clock, or four thirty or six fifteen? Why can't it be three minutes after five, or seventeen minutes before eight, or like that?"

24

"I don't know," I said. "It's a good question. We could try to work on it as a system. 'Hello, Jackson? I'll meet you at twenty-two and a half minutes after three under the big clock.'"

She laughed happily. "Something else," she said.

"I think the whole idea went out with railroad trains," I said.

"Railroad . . . ? Oh, you mean schedules! But there's airline schedules."

"Not the same," I said stubbornly.

"Oh, well, I don't know. I never went anywhere on a train."

The Benedict Canyon end of the hotel drive was clogged up, so I went on to Beverly Drive and got into it from there. It was a steady stream but the attendants were working fast and we got to the entrance at five o'clock on the nose. Somebody opened the door and Abigail Caccelli leaned over and gave me a quick kiss on the cheek.

"You're a doll," she said. "Be seeing you."

"I hope so," I said.

The attendant closed the car door, and I saw her disappear into a crowded lobby, the white leather skirt swaying nicely behind.

Whew! I thought. And then I thought, "Very cute." And by the time I got down the hotel drive and straightened out on Sunset again, heading for Hollywood, I was thinking, if she talks that freely with me, how does she talk to her director?

I met this guy, he's a detective, something else—he's working for my mother—it's about Peter, you know, Peter Rinaldi . . .

25

I drove to the vicinity of La Cienega and Melrose, because I hadn't had anything to eat since breakfast and there's a bar and grill there which is the closest thing I've been able to find in Los Angeles to what I was used to in Chicago. Before I went in, I got out my *Guide to the Streets of Los Angeles* and looked up Redgrave Avenue. There were two of them, but one was on the far edge of Pasadena, which seemed unlikely. The other was in Culver City. I went over the route mentally a couple of times, put the map away and went in and ordered a ham and cheese sandwich on rye and a bottle of beer. It was a good sandwich and I ordered a second one and finished the beer. When I left the place, the sun was setting, and when I got into Culver City it was dark, or that almost-dark which is California's concession to twilight.

The address I was looking for was on a run-down side street lined with single dwellings and motor courts. Number 2605 was a rear unit in a court built on three sides of a ragged grass plot. There was a sign reading: VACANCY —Bachelors—1-Bdrm.—62.50–75.00. A couple of shaggy dogs were wrestling on the grass. They paid me no mind as I made the trek from the street to the rear apartment.

I struck a match, looking for a name. There was no light inside the apartment. Under a doorbell in a small brass slot was the name: M. Armande. I rang the bell and nobody came. I hadn't heard the bell ring, so I opened the screen door and knocked on the wooden panel. Still no answer. There was a window beside the door and I closed the screen and tried to look inside, but the shade was drawn. I heard a buzzing sound behind me and turned to find a boy about eleven years old, fooling with a slot car racing model, spinning the wheels with the flat of his hand.

"You looking for Michele?" he said.

"A—yes. Michele Armande," I said.

He spun the wheels a couple of times. "She ain't home. I guess she went to work already."

"I see. Can you tell me where she works?"

"She's a waitress. Some place on National."

"You happen to know the name of the place?"

He shook his head, spun the wheels and turned to look at the dogs, who were growling and snapping at each other now.

"Well," I said, "is it like a restaurant or something?"

"Nah," the kid said, "it's just a place to drink."

"A beer place?"

He shrugged, watching the dogs. "It's by the bowling alley," he said. "It's sort of up a ways from the slot car place."

A door opened in the unit next door and a woman leaned out. "Roger, you come in here," she said.

The kid turned, spinning the wheels of the car against his palm, and went home. I left the motor court, got in the car and drove over to National Boulevard. It wasn't far.

It didn't take long to find the bowling alley, which was on a main corner. On the next corner was the slot car racing course. In between were two cocktail lounges and a beer joint called the Back Room. Working up from the slot car place, I went into the first cocktail lounge. Nobody in there had ever heard of Michele Armande.

Business was slack everywhere. In the second emporium, the bartender was polishing glasses at leisure. After thinking about it for a minute, he said he guessed there was a woman named Michele working at the Back Room. I thanked him and went in there.

Things were livelier in the Back Room than elsewhere, but it didn't look like a gold mine. Four guys were seated along the bar, and half a dozen others in booths sat against the opposite wall. They drank from pitchers mostly. In the rear was a pool table and a game in progress. Though there was a service setup in the middle of the bar, I saw no sign of a waitress. A group in one of the booths sang out for another pitcher, and the bartender drew and delivered the brew himself. I found an empty bar stool, settled on it and ordered a glass of the premium. It was foamy cold and nice. A flurry of orders kept the bartender so busy that five minutes passed before he got around to picking up my money.

"You could use a waitress," I said.

He made a face, then made my change and brought it back.

"He's got a waitress, huh, Harry?" said a customer on my right.

He laughed. Harry didn't feel like laughing. "That broad," he said. "Five times in two weeks she didn't show up."

"Well," the happy customer said, "she's probably busy at the studio." More boisterous laughter. "Brigitte Bardot the second," he said.

"Yeah," Harry said, "your grandmother."

"I bet the last time she was in a movie was in World War One. Remember those blimps used to hang up there —recon blimps?"

Laugh—he like to have fractured himself.

"Maybe she's sick," another customer said mildly.

"Sick drunk," Harry said. "I knew she was a lush the day she came in here. I said the other day, 'Look, baby, you know what a telephone is—you could call up?' "

A man with a pool cue came from the rear. "Cue ball's hung up," he said.

"Jiggle the table," Harry said.

"I did jiggle it. Everybody jiggled it."

"Goddamned—" Harry muttered, and went away to the pool table.

"I think I saw her in a picture last night," the soft-spoken customer said. "A real oldie, on the tube."

"Saw who?"

"Michele," he said. "I forgot the name of it. She had a French accent—she was good-looking. Not much of a part though."

"*Hollywood Canteen*," Happy Jack said. "Everybody was in that one."

"No it wasn't *Hollywood Canteen*."

Harry came back and washed a few glasses. "I wish she'd leave those two clowns at home," he said, "when she does come in. They bug me. Sit there, take up space, drink thirty cents worth of beer—"

"Hey, yeah," Laughing Boy said. "That's something else—two boy friends—"

"Boy friends," Harry said. "Probably a couple of bill collectors."

The happy one couldn't give up. "She's got to have two boy friends," he said. "It *takes* two—"

"Ah—you're full," Harry muttered.

"Speak of the devil," the quiet customer said.

Two men came into the tavern and walked to the street end of the bar. They were well set up, well dressed. One of them wore shades. The other one did the talking. He didn't move his mouth much, and after a minute I could see why. He had a skin graft job on the left side of his face. It was a pretty good job, as far as appearances went, but I could imagine it kept his face tight. You could trace the outline of the graft easily once you were onto it.

"Where's Michele?" he asked Harry.

Harry went on polishing the glasses. "She didn't show. I don't know why."

"She didn't come to work?"

"No," Harry said, "she didn't."

"She didn't call?"

"She never calls."

"What time was she due?" Scarface asked.

"An hour ago," Harry said.

"You heard nothing from her?"

"That's what I said."

Scarface and the one in the shades looked at each other, looked along the bar, turned and walked out, heavy on their heels.

"I don't like those guys," Happy Boy said. "They're some kind of bad guys."

"Like I said," Harry said. And to me he said, "Another beer?"

"No, thanks," I said, "I got to go."

When I got outside, the two heavyweights were entering a green Mustang parked half a block up the street. My car was in the opposite direction and there was no way in the world for me to reach it in time to follow them. So I didn't make the attempt.

I got into my car, circled the block, found no trace of the green Mustang, and headed back to Redgrave Avenue. I made a couple of wrong turns and it took me about ten minutes to find Michele Armande's apartment at the back of the court. Even before I left the car, I could see there was light in it.

I walked back there. The dogs were no longer cavorting

on the scrubby green. The boy with the slot car was nowhere in sight. Through the dusty screen I could see that Michele's door stood ajar. I rang the bell and this time I heard it ring, loud and clear. But still nobody came. I opened the screen, pushed at the door, which opened easily, and walked in. From a hallway leading to the rear of the apartment, Peter Rinaldi came into the living room.

His face was a dirty gray color, a smear on his naturally swarthy complexion. He wasn't steady on his feet. He looked at me without recognition and pointed with his thumb over his shoulder.

"In there—" he said.

I could tell by the way he looked, I didn't want to go there. Back in the hall, past where the kitchen must be, a door stood open with light beyond it. I didn't want to go. But I had a check in my pocket for a hundred and fifty dollars on Peter Rinaldi's behalf, and so I went, skirting him carefully because it looked as if he were about to fall over.

It wasn't a long trip. I got to the open door, turned right and walked into a bedroom. The bed was unmade. A pile of soiled clothes was heaped on a chair in one corner. A middle-aged woman, pretty well gone to soft flesh, was hanging by a silk scarf from the head frame of a double bed. She was wearing a chenille bathrobe. She had a soft, knitted slipper on her left foot; the right foot had lost its slipper. Her feet were resting on the floor and her knees were bent awkwardly. Her exposed foot was very white, like milk. Her hands were white. Her face had a bad color.

I got out my pocketknife, went to the bed and laid the back of my hand against her face, then against her neck.

She was cold, dead cold. But I sawed through the silk scarf anyway. Her body slipped down along the edge of the bed and thudded softly on the floor. I could see that the scarf was tightly knotted at the back of her neck. There was no evidence at a glance that her neck was broken. I checked her heartbeat and temperature again and knew that a try at resuscitation would be futile. I had had enough of the scene and I left the bedroom and went to the living room where Peter Rinaldi was standing as I had left him.

Footsteps pounded outside and in came Scarface and his friend with the shades. They filled the doorway for a second, then came on inside. Scarface, as before, was the spokesman.

"All right, where is she?" he said. "We're from the police."

I caught his eyes and held them. "No you're not," I said. I got out my wallet and flipped it open, then shut it and put it away. "But don't leave. I'd like to talk to you."

I started around Rinaldi toward them. They lingered for about half a heartbeat, then turned and piled out.

"Hold it!" I said, just to finish off the set, but they kept going, almost at a run.

Needless to say, I let them go.

3

I LOOKED at Rinaldi and he said, "You're that writer fellow . . . wanted to write about Mary . . . "

"I'm that fellow," I said, "but I'm not a writer."

"You're an officer?"

"No, that was for the benefit of the troops."

"Well, I—"

"Have you been here long?" I asked him.

He shook his head. "A few minutes. The door was open—unlocked."

"Was the light on when you came?"

"No. I turned it on. I had an appointment to come here."

"Yes, I saw the message."

"Oh," he said. "I see. Mary showed you?"

"Yes, she did. She feels you're in some sort of trouble."

His mouth twisted in what might have been a sardonic smile. I couldn't be sure. He was extremely tight.

"From the look of things," I said, "it wasn't an unreasonable conclusion on her part."

"Dear Mary," he said, very gently.

I gave him a short time to think about dear Mary and then I said, "Is there anything you want to tell me?"

He opened his mouth, closed it and shook his head. "No—I can't make any sense out of anything—"

"Because," I said, "I'll have to call the cops in a few minutes and they'll be curious and all that."

"Yes, I know."

"Will you tell me this much," I said, "did you kill her?"

He looked at me, too long, and he said, "No, I didn't."

That's nice, I thought. That helps.

Hello, Lieutenant Shapiro? Hi ya, Lou old boy, look I seem to have this corpse—yeah, there was a guy here but he said he didn't do it, so I said why don't you run along home—

"Well," I said to Rinaldi, "how did you get here? You drove?"

"Yes, I'm parked out in back, there's a space—"

"Feel up to driving home?"

"I don't know . . . I guess so . . . I'm shaky."

"Drive carefully," I said. "Think about what you're doing every minute. Don't stop in the middle of the block and don't pass up any signals. Stay off the freeways."

"I understand."

"Those two guys who were here," I said, "you ever see them before?"

He started to shake his head, then thought better of it. "Yes," he said, "one day . . . they were waiting for me at home . . . at Mary's . . ."

"What did they want from you?"

"Well, they said they had some deal for me, a picture deal, and would I talk to them about it."

"Some picture deal?"

"I don't know exactly what was involved in it—they were rather vague."

34

"Did they mention Michele Armande in connection with the deal?"

"Yes, her name came up. But as I said—"

"Then that could have been the meaning of that message you got—'Last chance Monday,' and so forth."

"Probably, yes."

I nodded. It was time for him to go. I didn't really want him to go, because then I would have to go back to the grubby business of checking out the dead lady in the bedroom. But it was time for Peter Rinaldi to remove himself from the scene.

"Let me go out with you," I said, "—make sure those spooks aren't hanging around."

"I don't know why they—"

"I don't either," I said, "but they act funny."

By the time we got to the small parking area behind the court, he was steady on his feet. The parking entrance was off an alley that ran through to a main thoroughfare.

"Roll up the windows, lock the doors and keep it moving," I said. "I won't mention to the cops that you were here. But I'll want to talk to you later."

"Of course," he said.

He got away smoothly enough. I watched till he had made the street and disappeared, then went back to Michele Armande's apartment. It was lonely as a tomb in an abandoned cemetery. There was a telephone in the living room, on an end table beside a sofa. I studied it longingly. I could call Lou Shapiro and turn the job over to its rightful heirs. I could get out of it that way.

Matter of fact, I thought, it's my legal duty to call Shapiro, at once!

And if Shapiro finds anything useful, he'll tell me about

it. Like if he finds anything that might involve my client, he'll consult me first.

Sure he will.

I closed the front door against possible nosy neighbors, such as small boys with slot cars, and spent some time in the living room. It didn't appear to be much lived in. There was a film of dust on the furniture, maybe two, three days old. The room contained no such item as a desk or bookcase, in which interesting exhibits might have been stored. There was a small table just inside the door and a few pieces of mail had been dropped on it. They were all recent, within the last two or three days. There were a gas bill and an electric bill, a form letter from a stockbroker, all addressed to a Patricia White at this address. There was a postcard, similarly addressed, but with no message of any kind, postmarked North Pine, California. The postmark was three days old, and the picture was of a rustic mountain lodge set among high trees.

Where did I get the name Michele Armande? I thought.

You got it off the nameplate on the front door, I told myself. There was the initial "M" and when the kid said "Michele," you concluded that was her name. And that was the name of the waitress at the Back Room all right. So who is Patricia White? Michele's roommate?

But there was no sign of a double occupancy.

I lifted the cushions on the sofa and found some debris, a few bobby pins, a penny, a piece of Kleenex. Under the cushion of the overstuffed chair there wasn't even that much, not even a penny. There was one drawer in the end table under the telephone, but all it contained was a telephone book. In the narrow hall leading to the rear, the first door opened on a coat closet. There were three cloth coats on hangers and a leather jacket. They were all the same size. I went through the pockets and found some chewing gum, more bobby pins, a couple of match covers advertising savings and loan institutions, and a little change, nickels and dimes.

The next door opened on the kitchen. A trash basket was overflowing and there were half a dozen empty whiskey bottles on the floor beside it. In the sink were a few unwashed dishes, not many, and on the stove, one cooking pot containing what looked like chili.

I emptied the trash basket onto the floor and pawed through the mess. Aside from a couple of throwaway newspapers, it consisted of food wrappers and used paper towels and beer cans. I set the basket up, refilled it, rinsed my hands at the sink and dried them on a paper towel. I tossed the towel into the trash basket, then picked it out and put it in my pocket.

There remained the bedroom and the bath, which was at the far end of the hall, straight on. It was small—room to turn around if you stood ramrod straight. The tub and shower were a tight cubicle of about 24 by 54 inches, which I believe is the smallest unit of that sort legally available in California. Two pairs of sheer panty hose hung over the shower curtain rod. The tub was clean and dry.

That took care of the innocuous places and I had no more excuse for avoiding the bedroom and the corpse. Time had begun to push at me. I didn't know Peter Rinaldi at all well. I couldn't predict what he might do before he reached home. He might have stopped somewhere already and called the police. And then those other two—whoever they were.

The corpse herself got short shrift from me. There was nothing to be done about her, and there was little I could learn by examination. She was out of my field. I did take another look at the knotted scarf around her neck. It had been drawn tighter, probably, than she could have done herself. It was a bad way to hang yourself anyway—awkward, not enough drop. It seemed unlikely that she had done it herself.

The clothing piled on the chair appeared to be a collection for the dry cleaner. It was mostly dresses, blouses, a knit suit with skirt and blouse. No pockets in anything and nothing lying around loose under the pile on the chair seat. More dresses hung in a half-open closet. There were also some western shirts and two pairs of well-worn blue jeans hanging on a hook. Lots of pockets, front and back. They contained, with one exception, the same bag of odds and ends I had found elsewhere—bobby pins, some matches, an empty cigaret package. The exception consisted of a few dried pine needles, such as a pocket might scoop up while seated under a tree. I rubbed a few of them between my fingers and they were very old, dry and crumbly. I put them back where I had found them.

There was nothing else, no strong box with private papers, no wallet with credit cards, bank references, nothing like that. It was possible the lady didn't own such things. There are people in the world who live on a cash basis, day by day. They are usually poor people.

With a kind of nod to the dead lady, I went out of the room. I reached for the telephone, changed my mind and passed it. Too much explaining to do if I waited at the scene for the first cop to come along. Shapiro—all right, but he wouldn't be the first.

At the table in the entry I had another look at the postcard from North Pine. The lack of a message was singular, but not inspiring. A lot of people send such cards as a way of letting someone know they arrived somewhere safely. Some people don't like to write things down.

I opened the front door, left it off the latch and took another look at the name card in the brass slot. I lit a match and looked at it closely. It was clean and fresh-looking, as if it had been put up within the last day or so.

I went to my car, drove a few blocks and pulled up at a streetside phone booth. I put in a call to the cops. Lieutenant Shapiro wasn't in, so I gave the message to a sergeant named Hennessy.

"Are you at the scene?" he asked.

"No. I'm heading for my office. Lieutenant Shapiro knows where it is."

"You'll be there?"

"Yeah, I live there."

"Okay," he said.

It had taken some searching to find the combination apartment and office I wanted. It was on a Hollywood side street, north of the Boulevard and east of Vine. There were three other tenants in the building, two of them lawyers. The third was a young lady astrologer named Gilda. I had the whole of the third floor, of three. It was a penthouse.

The elevator opened on a front hall that ran the width of the building. The office door was first on the right at the east end of the hall. On the door were the words: Private Investigator—Please Ring Bell. (Few people did; most knocked.) The office was spacious and contained a desk, several chairs, a couch, a couple of filing cabinets and a bookcase with glass doors. It was full of books that had been left by a previous tenant, and I had not got around to reading any of them yet.

Farther along the hall was another door, which opened on my living room. It had windows overlooking the Gower Street ramp of the Hollywood Freeway. So I had two choices. I could use the go-home door or the office door. It kept life exciting. There was also a connecting door from the office to the living room. I also had a back exit, by way of a flight of stairs. The back door opened on an alley, across which was parking space for the tenants' cars. All in all it was an old building and nothing fancy, but the appliances worked and the price was right.

It was about nine fifteen and I went into the office. I had barely got the door shut behind me and was picking up the telephone to check in with my answering service, when the doorbell rang. I let the answering service wait and opened the door. Outside in the hall stood my glamour girl acquaintance, Abigail Caccelli. With her was a tallish, heavy-set guy in a black turtleneck and love beads, wearing oversize, owl-like glasses and carrying about fifty years of age.

"Hello . . . uh . . . you," Abigail said. "Can we come in? This is the detective, Mac," she said to the big guy, "this is my director, Ed Fogel."

"Come in," I said.

My hunch paid off all the way, I was thinking. She must have spilled every word we exchanged during that ride to the hotel.

I showed them places to sit and offered drinks. Abigail shook her head firmly. Mr. Fogel at first declined, then, before I could sit down, allowed as he might, just a short one. I fixed him a whiskey and soda and poured a short slug for myself to keep him from being embarrassed.

"How's the picture going?" I asked.

"Great—" Abigail said, "just wonderful. It's the most exciting thing I ever did in my life!"

Fogel shrugged. "It's okay," he said.

There came one of those total pauses. It had a duration of at least twenty seconds, and I could come up with no more small talk fill-in.

"What can I do for you?" I asked.

Fogel looked at Abigail. Abigail was looking at a picture on the wall beyond where I sat at my desk. It was a picture of a bridge in some foreign country—Italy, I think —and I had inherited it along with the books.

"That's terrible," she said. "Remind me to get you some good pictures."

"I'd appreciate it," I said.

"I know some really great artists—groovy."

"If the price is right—" I said.

But that was all the time we had for art.

"Listen," Abigail said, "I told Ed about you and Peter. See, Ed has known Peter for years and naturally he was interested—"

Fogel decided to give some point to the discussion. "Peter Rinaldi was a good actor," he said. "Could always depend on him, never had to tell him anything twice."

"When was the last time he worked?" I asked.

He scratched his head some. "About ten years ago," he said. "A picture called *Slow Poison*—suspense thing, we lost our shirt. But he had a good bit. Anyway, Abby told me he was in some kind of trouble and I figured, if I can do anything about it—"

In other words, I was thinking, you would like to know what's going on here.

"Well," I said, "I can't tell you much. I don't know

much. As Abby probably told you, I was at her mother's house today and she talked about it and she doesn't know much either. We're just sort of looking into it."

There was another of those pauses, more pregnant this time. I didn't feel like breaking into it.

"There was something about a woman being murdered," Ed Fogel said.

"There was?" I said.

He looked into space, knowing he had jumped the old gun.

"You've been in touch with somebody?" I asked.

He shook his head vigorously. It made his jowls wiggle. "No. I just—I don't know."

"Well," I said, "as I said, I don't know either. Only what I told you."

"But—" Abigail started, and Fogel shook his head at her.

"You say you'd like to do something for Peter Rinaldi," I said. "If there were something, what would you have in mind? Have you got a job for him?"

"Well, not this minute, but I keep trying, you know. No, it was just that if he's in some kind of trouble, you know—"

I looked at the fair Abigail, not without pleasure, and at Fogel the director, with not much interest, and I said, "I don't know what to say. I don't know whether Peter is in trouble or not. So I can't say what might be done."

Fogel knew when an interview had ended. He got up abruptly, nodding to me and beckoning Abigail. "Let's go, baby." And to me he said, "I meant what I said. If there's anything I can do, you can always reach me at the studio."

"I appreciate it," I said, "and I'm sure Peter does too."

At the door, Abigail turned and flashed me a sunshine smile. "Well—bye now," she said.

"So long, Abigail," I said, "I hope we'll see each other soon."

"Oh sure," she said.

They went away. I dialed my answering service and there had been several calls which didn't seem urgent, and then there had been a call from Lieutenant Shapiro —recently. I dialed his personal number at headquarters. It rang a long time and finally something clicked and the line opened from the switchboard. I said I was returning Lieutenant Shapiro's call.

"Yes," the switchboard girl said, "he wants to talk to you as soon as possible. Will you be there a few minutes?"

"I'll make it a point," I said.

"I'll get in touch with him and he will call."

I thanked her and hung up.

I was in the bathroom, washing my face and hands, when his call came. I took it in the bedroom. It was dark in there.

"Mac speaking," I said. "Lieutenant—?"

"Yeah," Shapiro said. "About that corpse you called about—Redgrave Avenue."

"Yes," I said.

"Where is it?"

"Where—? It's in the bedroom—rear apartment, number twenty-six-oh-five—"

"No," he said.

"No what?"

"That's where I am now," he said. "No corpse, no sign of such a thing."

I reached out mechanically and switched on the bedroom light. It didn't help.

"Well—" I said, "what do you want me to do?"

"Don't know," he said frankly. "Anybody else see it, anybody besides you?"

"Yeah—couple of guys—"

"Who?"

"I don't know—wait, I don't know if they really saw it."

Peter Rinaldi, I was thinking, where are you now that I need you?

Lou Shapiro let a short time pass. It seemed like a long, long time. "Mac—" he said.

"Yeah, Lieutenant."

"You goofed. You screwed up."

That firmed me a little. "You want to hear my side of the story?"

"I'd like to."

"Where?"

"You name it."

"All right, there's a beer joint called the Back Room, on National Boulevard. That's where she worked."

"Where who worked?"

"The—corpse!"

"Okay," he said, with far too much condescension. "I guess it's as good a place as any."

I hung up, switched off the light, got into my jacket and went out into the ambiguous Hollywood night.

4

LIEUTENANT LOU Shapiro was sitting in a booth with a tired-looking glass of beer in front of him, gazing into space with his mournful eyes. The joint was busier than it had been earlier, but not much. The bartender, Harry, had found a relief man and was doing the room-side service himself, not really enjoying it. I slid into the space opposite the Lieutenant and held my peace till he granted me notice.

"Go ahead, talk," he said.

"May I order a glass of beer?"

"Sure."

I got Harry's attention and ordered a glass. When he brought it I said to him, "Do you have a couple of minutes?" He looked around, shrugged and sat down. "I guess so," he said.

"I was here earlier," I said.

"I remember."

"This is Lieutenant Shapiro, Los Angeles police."

Harry looked harassed. "What's the beef?" he said.

Shapiro shook his head. "No beef," he said, "anyway not with you."

I accepted the hint. "Harry—" I said, "did Michele Armande ever show up for work tonight?"

"No," Harry said.

"And she didn't call in?"

"No."

"You know where Michele Armande lives?"

He moved around some, cast his eye over the joint and returned to us.

"Listen," he said, "I've got nothing for that broad, but if there's a beef—"

Patiently, Shapiro shook his head. "No beef against her," he said.

"Well, she lives over on Redgrave, not far—"

"Twenty-six-oh-five Redgrave?"

"Something like that. I don't know without looking it up."

"All right," I said, "thanks, Harry. There's one other thing. You remember that when I was here, two guys came in asking about her?"

He nodded.

"And there was some conversation at the bar about them, like they were mysterious and I think somebody even said they were like bad guys, and like that."

"Yeah—those guys—yeah."

"And you said they were in the habit of coming in when Michele was working and hanging around, waiting, coming and going with her."

"Yeah, they were always hanging around."

"Do you know who they are?"

"No," he said.

"You know their names?"

"Huh-uh. I know nothing about them."

"You didn't like them."

He shrugged and looked around the room. "They bugged me. I don't know why. They just bugged me."

"Did you ever see them outside of the place here, anywhere outside it?"

"No, I never——"

"What I'm getting at is what kind of a car they drove or anything like that. Tonight I saw them in a green Mustang."

"I never saw a Mustang. One night I remember, they were leaving with Michele and they went out the back way. I happened to be out there for a minute, dumping some trash, and they had some kind of a panel truck. They drove away in it."

"A panel truck? Was there a name on it, a business name, anything like that?"

"I don't remember if there was or not."

I wished he could remember. "How long had Michele been working for you?"

"Too long," he said, "about four, five days."

"Is that all? I had an idea it had been a long time."

"No, it just seemed long to me."

"Okay, Harry, I don't want to keep you. Thanks."

"Sure, okay, you want another beer?"

I looked at Shapiro, who shook his head. "Not right now," I said.

Harry went away. Shapiro was gazing at me sadly. "Where do you go from here?" he said.

"I'll try to tell like it was," I said. "It was like this."

And I told him everything about it, except about Peter Rinaldi, who, regrettably, was my only supporting witness. When I finished he brooded into his stale beer and rubbed his black eyebrows as if they itched, which no doubt they did.

"You say you cut her down from the bedpost," he said. "Did you try to revive her at all?"

"No, too late obviously. She was cold. There was nothing working in her."

He thought about that. "So it's not likely that she came to, untied the thing around her neck and went away somewhere."

"It is extremely unlikely."

"So you were hanging around there, cutting her down and all, and these two fellows came in."

"Yeah, but I was in the living room then. They didn't go in the bedroom while I was there."

"And they tried to pull a law officer bit on you and you turned it back on them and they beat it. Is that the way it happened?"

"That's right."

"What time was this?" he asked without warning.

I swallowed some beer the wrong way and choked on it. When I recovered, Shapiro was watching me. He had me in a small squeeze. If I made the discovery time too early, he would be asking what I did with all that time before I called in. Peter was my only honest explanation, and Peter had to be kept out of it.

"I don't know exactly," I said, "around eight thirty, a quarter to nine."

He nodded absently. "Who were you working for?" he asked. "Who was your client?"

"Can't say."

"It wasn't Michele Armande?"

"No, not Michele."

He sat back in the seat, laid both hands flat on the table and sighed. "Well, I guess I'm nowhere," he said.

"You know I've been around too long to pull a thing like that on you," I said, "a put-on like that."

He studied me briefly. "Sure," he said, "and you've been around long enough to know you should stay on the scene of such a thing after you call in."

"Ordinarily I would," I said, "but I had an urgent appointment in Hollywood. I just couldn't."

He looked at me some more and then he started to get up.

"What now?" I said.

"Look at it this way," he said. "There's nothing I can do. There's no crime, no evidence of one. If she doesn't turn up in a few days, and people begin wondering why, then maybe I could take what you say and the fact that she's missing and make something out of it. But right now —nothing, Mac, nothing at all."

"All right," I said, "I'll walk out with you."

He was on his feet. I slid out of the booth and we headed for the street. I almost bumped my nose against his shoulder when he stopped suddenly just short of the door. He hovered there for a beat and a half, then went on. As nearly as I could tell, he had paused to look at a guy who was sitting alone at the end of the bar, a smallish, dapper-looking guy with a nice manicure, out of place in a neighborhood tavern like the Back Room. But Shapiro didn't do anything about it, and when I caught up with him he was muttering under his breath.

"I beg your pardon?" I said.

"What? . . . Oh, I was just wondering what Caccelli was doing in a joint like this."

"Caccelli?"

"Joe Caccelli. 'Little Joe' they call him."

49

"Who is he?"

"Little Joe? He's a guy, a pint-size prod, wears elevator shoes and fingernail polish. His tab at the barbershop for one visit would keep a workingman like me, or you, in New York steaks and good wine for a week. Take any week, the working stiff would be well-fed and likewise Little Joe. But Caccelli would also have a nice haircut."

"I got it, I think," I said.

"The reason it was a shock to see him," Shapiro said, "is because he's such a social climber, coming up in the world, the upper world, that is. Married to an actress, Abigail Dane. She's the daughter of the silent movie star Mary Dane. You remember her."

"I remember."

"I understand she's a lousy actress—Abigail, I mean."

"Well—the name may help."

"I suppose so. Well, I spent enough time, Mac. If you get anything on this . . . uh . . . corpus delicti, give me a ring. But the next time, stay there."

"Yes, Lieutenant."

"So long for now."

He walked away down the street and I looked back at the joint for a few seconds, but decided against monkeying around with Joe Caccelli, and pretty soon I got to my car and started home. I felt low in spirit, and somewhere along the way I pulled up at an ice cream parlor and ate a hot fudge sundae. It soothed my palate but did nothing for my spirit. I drove on home, put the car in the slot and went up to the office by the back stairs. There were some desk chores to be done and I started to work on them, but I was too dispirited and finally I turned off the light, made sure the door was locked and went all the way home by way of the connecting door. I was in my pants, shirt-less, when the office bell rang. I tried to ignore it, but it rang again and I pulled on a sweater and went to see who was there.

It was a grizzled, dried-up guy wearing a cap on which were embroidered the words: Red Ball Messenger Service. He had a small envelope in his hand and a delivery receipt book. He handed me the envelope and held out the book and the pencil.

"Sign here," he said.

"Am I sure I want this?" I said.

He shrugged. "You don't have to take it," he said.

"Do I have to pay for it?"

"No, it's paid. You want to sign?"

I turned the envelope over. Engraved on the flap in dignified script was the name: Peter Rinaldi.

"I'll sign," I said, and I did.

I gave him a quarter and he nodded and went away. I closed the door, slit the envelope and took out a piece of notepaper bearing the handwritten message:

"Michele Armande died eight or nine years ago, some-where up north." It was signed, "P. R."

I put it back in the envelope, stuck it in a desk drawer, turned out the light again and went to bed. It took a while to get to sleep. The ice cream didn't sit well.

5

AT SEVEN in the morning I got up and made some coffee, which didn't sit much better than the ice cream, though it did get me through a shower and shave. At eight o'clock I called Peter Rinaldi at the home of Mary Dane. Rinaldi answered the phone.

"About your message—" I said.

"Yes—I sent you a message—"

He sounded old and tired.

"I guess we had better talk things over," I said.

"Yes, I suppose so."

"Your place or mine?"

"Not here."

"All right. My place, as soon as you can make it."

I gave him the address before I remembered he already had it.

"Have you had breakfast?" I asked.

He laughed in a cackling way and hung up. I drank some more of the coffee, boiled a couple of eggs and got them down while checking out the *L. A. Times*. There was no such story as: "Michele Armande—or the Vanishing Corpse," and I concluded that Lou Shapiro had quashed it by putting down the call as a false alarm. Or possibly there had been no reporter to pick up the call in the first place.

I opened a telephone book and looked for Joe Caccelli. He was not listed in the Central Los Angeles section, nor in any of the outlying areas from Pasadena to the beach, nor from Redondo Beach to the far reaches of the San Fernando Valley.

I called Lou Shapiro at headquarters and he happened to be in.

"Last night," I said, "you mentioned a Joe Caccelli."

"He was in that tavern, yeah."

"What does Joe Caccelli do, besides marry young actresses and get his hair cut?"

"I don't know everything he does, but for one thing, he's got a string of vending machines."

"Jukeboxes?"

"Including jukeboxes. Also stamps, gumballs, sandwiches—"

"What's the firm name?"

"Uh . . . let's see . . . there's more than one. The big one, I guess, would be Star-Line Enterprises."

"Star-Line. In L. A.?"

"Yeah. Down in the wholesale district. I'd have to look up the street and number."

"Never mind. Thanks, Lieutenant."

He beat me out of the hangup. "Why do you ask?" he said.

"I don't know. Just curious."

"In the market for a jukebox?"

"No, but I run into a lot of people. It's nice to have odd information like this."

"What's the connection between Joe Caccelli and Michele Armande?"

He remembered names good. He had done his research.

"If any," I said, "I don't know."

"You don't know?"

"No, Lieutenant."

"Are you guessing?"

"Not out loud."

There was a lengthy pause. I wanted to hang up, but I was in no position to be rude to Shapiro.

"All right, Mac," he said finally, "watch your step around Caccelli."

"Sure, Lou."

Still he wouldn't hang up. "Caccelli read a lot of history. The books he read were all about making it the hard way. By hard way you know what I mean."

"I know."

"There are people around town—freaks—that will do anything for twenty bucks."

"Sure."

"I mean anything, Mac. For twenty bucks."

"Okay."

"So, you for instance can take care of yourself. But there are those who can't."

A vibration went into my ear and found its way down the middle of my back.

"Yeah?" I said.

"Take somebody like Peter Rinaldi," Lou said.

"Whoever he is," I said.

"Uh-huh. He's Michele Armande's husband."

"Oh," I said.

"So long, Champ," he said, and hung up.

"Wait—" I said.

But Lou was gone.

I looked up Star-Line Enterprises and found it listed,

with an address on Santa Fe Street. I was making a note of it when the door opened and Gilda, my astrologer, danced in. She looked very cute in her cat-eye, tinted glasses, in a swirly, soft-looking dress and her bare feet. She was by far the prettiest tenant in the building, and I planned to marry her one day after she grew up a little more.

"It's a day for you to watch your step," she said, shaking a slender finger at me.

I nodded. "Man that keep eyes on ground," I said, "often get hit in back of head with stardust."

"Oh dear—" she said.

She was always saying "Oh dear." From her it was cute.

"Don't go too far away," I said, "but I've got a client coming in a few minutes."

"All right," she said. "See you later."

I threw her a kiss and she danced away.

Another thing about her, she couldn't walk like other people for some reason. She was always skipping or dancing.

I dialed Mary Dane's number and she came on. I asked for Peter Rinaldi.

"I'm sorry," she said, "you just missed him. He said he had to go downtown."

"It's all right. I expect to see him later anyway. I was wondering, though, have you seen any more loiterers in the neighborhood—such as the two men who came to see Peter?"

"No, nobody. Can you tell me anything?"

I gave it a second's thought. "No, I'm afraid not yet. But soon, I hope."

"All right, thank you, Mac."

"Thank you," I said and hung up.

She was a nice client. A real lady. I hoped I would never have to hold out on her for longer than a few hours. At the moment, however, it appeared that Peter Rinaldi was in something up to his eyebrows. I was working for him as well as for Mary Dane. I seemed also to be working for Lieutenant Lou Shapiro of the L. A. police—but that kind of work is always in the game.

Rinaldi showed up around nine thirty. He looked about the same as when I had seen him the night before, well-groomed, composed, with the nicely balanced bearing of the trained actor. His eyes were a little red and I assumed he hadn't enjoyed much sleep lately. I offered him some coffee, which he accepted gratefully, and let him get into it some before I put him on the rack.

"Anything you'd like to tell me?" I asked.

He blinked slowly at his coffee cup and shook his head. "I don't think so. If I could—but what I told you last night is all I know."

"Your message—about Michele Armande having died some years ago."

"Yes," he said, "that was what I remembered later—after I left you."

"How would you happen to know a thing like that? Had you known Michele Armande in the past?"

"Well . . . somewhat. She was in pictures for a while —bits."

He was very tight and he would have to be pried open. I hoped I could do it without spilling too much juice. He would need as much juice as he could contain.

"There's something I have to tell you," I said. "I'm in a bad bind. You may or may not be in it with me."

His eyes sharpened. I thought I saw behind them the

56

brimming of his undisclosed secrets, but I couldn't be sure.

"Yes?" he said.

"The dead body of Michele Armande has disappeared. It was gone when I met the police near the scene—not long after you started home."

His response was unexpected. "How long after?" he said.

"Well—why do you ask?"

"I don't know. It just seems that such a thing would take time."

"Probably about half an hour. I went home and heard from the police maybe an hour and a half later."

"I see," he said, and that was all the suggestion he had.

"While I was at home," I said, "Abigail came to see me, accompanied by her director, Ed Fogel."

"Yes?" he said.

He was good at saying "Yes" and "I see." I could figure he had a bigger vocabulary, if only I could find a way to tap it.

"I got a strong impression that Fogel had already learned about the killing."

With quite a lot of deliberation, Rinaldi finished his coffee, got up and set it on a neutral spot on the corner of my desk and sat down again. He eased the crease in his pants, crossed one leg over the other and leaned back in his chair. He ran one hand back over his smooth bald head and then folded his hands together in his lap.

"Yes," he said. "I called Ed Fogel."

It was my turn. "I see," I said.

Some time passed creakingly.

"Years ago," he said, "Ed Fogel and Michele Armande were lovers."

"I see."

"And . . . I thought he ought to know . . . that she was dead."

"So you called him and told him."

"Yes. You can trust Ed Fogel. He's all right."

Sure, I was thinking. I can trust anybody some of the time and everybody all of the time and nobody much of the time—

"What was his reaction?" I asked. "I mean, when you told him she was dead, how did he take it?"

"Well . . . Ed is pretty cool."

Some cool, I thought, the way he came on with me. "How long ago?" I asked.

"I beg your pardon?"

"How long ago were Ed Fogel and Michele Armande lovers?"

"Some time ago—fifteen years."

I got up from where I had been sitting, filled my coffee cup, walked around and drank some of it.

"Rinaldi," I said, "one or both of us are in some kind of trouble. I don't know what it is. I don't know what it means. I know I don't like it. If you can help me, I'll accept the help. If you can't—or for some reason don't want to—you had better get out of here and let me do whatever I can on my own."

I was close to being exasperated, but I admired his cool.

"I don't think I know what you mean," he said.

The trouble with that was, if he knew as much as I was beginning to suspect he knew, he also knew I wasn't in much real trouble. All I had to do was to call Lou Shapiro and tell him I was through worrying about Michele Armande, and he would rib me for a while and that would be the end of it. Only—

How did Rinaldi know that?

"How well did you know Michele Armande yourself?" I asked him.

The only sign I had that he was beginning to crack was an opening and closing of his mouth before the words came out. "I was married to her," he said.

I said, "Oh," because suddenly I preferred it to "I see."

"But that isn't of any importance really," he said. "It was just a legal thing. We never lived together."

"Well, all right. But you were married to her."

"Yes."

"And later divorced?"

There was a hell of a pause. "No," he said.

"You're still married to her—that is, if she were alive, you would be her husband?"

"I guess so."

"What was the legal thing?"

"I'd rather not say."

"Well, was it for her benefit, or yours?"

"I don't . . . mostly hers, I should say."

I sat down at my desk and brooded. "You thought Michele Armande was dead," I said. "I mean, you thought she had been dead for some time."

"That's correct."

He was going "Correct" and "I see" on me again.

"Then it must have been something of a surprise to you when you found her in that apartment last night."

"It was indeed."

"You had no warning of it at all?"

"No, none."

The exasperation was building up in me again. I was getting nowhere. It was maybe time to shift ground. But with Rinaldi, what could I hope for?

"What does Joe Caccelli have to do with it?" I asked.

That did something. Not much, but a little. He blinked —twice.

"Joe Caccelli?" he said. "I have no idea."

"Joe Caccelli is married to Abigail—Mary Dane's daughter."

"Yes, of course."

"How did Joe Caccelli meet Abigail?"

"Meet her?"

"Yeah, how did he get in with somebody like Abigail and Mary Dane? A minor hoodlum like him."

His face changed. He moved around in his chair. He didn't like the way it was going. I had hit him.

"I wasn't aware he was a . . . hoodlum," he said.

I wasn't either, but there was a chance of it and the suggestion seemed to be paying off.

"He's a nickel and dime hustler," I said. "How did he get next to a girl like Abigail?"

He squirmed some more. He didn't like this part of it.

"Maybe they went to the same college or something," I said.

He exerted enough counterforce on his own reactions to achieve momentary composure. "I helped arrange some screen tests—auditions, that sort of thing—for Abigail," he said. "Caccelli, I believe, met her at the studio."

"That would be Ed Fogel's studio?"

He nodded. "Universal," he said. "Ed rents space there."

"Did Abigail ever have any auditions anywhere else?"

He hesitated, shook his head. "No, not that I know of," he said.

"Caccelli hung around the studio?" I said. "Why? What was in it for him—aside from Abigail?"

"I don't know. I think he had some money in some of Fogel's productions."

"Did Caccelli know Michele Armande?"

"I suppose he did, before he married Abigail. He was around the studio, and Michele would be in and out."

"And she was Fogel's mistress."

"Oh no—you couldn't say that. Not in the recent past. It was some years ago."

"And then she died."

He nodded, uncertain now.

"And then she died again last night, is that it?"

He shrugged helplessly. We had completed the circle, and I knew little more than I had known in the beginning. Come to think of it, what I knew was less like knowledge than like the fragments of a torn-up movie gossip column, vintage ten years previous.

"Mr. Rinaldi," I said, "did Michele Armande come back from the dead and put the arm on you?"

He made a comprehensive surge in his chair and shook his head vigorously. "No," he said, "nothing like that."

"But somebody put the arm on you, in some way. A couple of handy boys from somewhere. The two who spent half a day waiting for you at Mary Dane's house."

"That was another matter altogether."

"Yes," I said, "you told me—it was about a picture deal."

"Yes," he said.

I gave some thought to pressing him again about why

he had married Michele in the first place, and while I was thinking about it, the telephone rang.

"Yeah," I said into it.

The voice on the other end was cool and confident, low-pitched, nonvibrant. "You are the private eye called Mac?" it said.

"Sometimes," I said.

"Joe Caccelli speaking."

"All right," I said.

"I want to talk to you—some business."

"Your place or mine?"

"Whatever's right."

"I'll be in and out. How about your place—eleven thirty?"

"Sure. Here's the address."

He gave me a street and number. It wasn't his business address. It was west side—Beverly Hills or Bel Air. I wrote it down.

"Okay," I said.

We hung up simultaneously. I looked at Rinaldi for a long thirty seconds.

"I guess I'd better get to work," I said. "Keep in touch. I'll let you know how things go."

"Very good," he said.

He got up rather briskly for a man of his age and he was at the door before he looked back, as if by afterthought, to say, "And thank you."

"Okay," I said, "stay out of trouble."

He nodded and went out. I wiped some coffee drainage off the desk, put the pot and cups in the kitchen sink, washed my hands and left the office. It felt good to be outside in the sweet, hot sunshine.

6

By the time I got to Beverly Hills, the sun was hotter and less sweet. I stopped and shed my jacket before making the climb up one of the more exclusive canyons toward the place to which Joe Caccelli had summoned me. The house stood on its own hill, and the drive mounted sharply from the road. There were parking slots on the level at the top. One of them housed Abigail's red Jaguar, and in another stood a black Continental about half a mile long. I slid my year-old Impala in beside the Jaguar and reached for my jacket, wondering whether the presence of Abigail's car indicated that she would be with us.

Probably not, I thought. Probably indicates the thing won't run.

The house was ranch style, unostentatious, surrounded by a lot of trees and shrubbery. All was on one level. Much of the wall space was glass, but it was all obscure, admitting light without vision. The entrance was a high, double-paneled door in Chinese red with a black iron knocker in the shape of a cat's paw. There was also a bell, which I punched lightly. I waited not longer than half a minute and the door opened on a slightly built male Oriental in a white jacket. He might have been twenty-five or he might have been sixty. His teeth were good, those that showed anyway, which could have been a sign of youth.

"My name is Mac," I said. "I have an appointment with Mr. Caccelli."

He bowed a little, not deeply, and stood back to let me in. I couldn't hear him close the door behind me, but I knew it had been done by the change in the light.

"Sit down, please," he said, indicating an arrangement of chairs and a sectional sofa that filled a third of a spacious living room. There was plenty of light, but it felt funny to look at the windows and not see anything through them.

What does he do if he just has to look outside? I wondered. Of course, I guess some people never do.

The house boy disappeared and I sat there. There were some magazines on a coffee table—*Life, Newsweek, Esquire*—and copies of the current issues of *Variety* and *Hollywood Reporter*. The rug was white shag, and a recent cigaret burn showed near my right shoe. I moved my foot to cover it.

Little Joe Caccelli entered from a hallway. It was the first time I had seen him on his feet and the nickname suddenly made literal sense. He stood about five feet five in his high-heeled shoes. He wouldn't have been much taller than Abigail, who was a buxom chick. His proportions were all right, enough shoulder, not much waist, legs and arms the right length. He wore a mod paisley jacket over a white sport shirt and a pair of bell-bottom pants of a zigzag black and white pattern. Maybe he figured it gave him extra height.

"I'm Caccelli," he said, and stuck out his hand.

I shook hands with him. What the hell.

64

"I'm Mac."

"Yeah, I heard about you."

"From who?" I said.

"Here and there," he said. "You came out of Chicago."

"Once," I said.

He sat down across the coffee table from me and the house boy appeared from nowhere.

"Something to drink?" Caccelli asked.

"Too early for me, thanks," I said.

"Coffee?"

"Nothing, thanks. You go ahead."

"I'm all right. I'll get to the point."

The house boy disappeared. Without looking, Caccelli seemed to know when he was gone.

"Look," he said, "I'm in the vending machine business. I'm opening up a new territory in San Diego, moving in with jukeboxes and a thing they call a "Flick-O-Mat"— instant movies, you know? It's a thing with a screen, like the tube, and you stick a quarter in it and these short flicks come up on the screen, with music. In color. It's a pretty good machine."

"I see," I said, wondering where I had heard that before.

"So," he said, "I got a guy down there running the thing for me, guy named Goldblatt. Hell of a salesman—I've known him to place four jukeboxes a day when he's hot. He's been all right on the new machine, too. But lately—"

He paused and looked toward one of the opaque windows. He had a slight twist in his nose and his eyes had a grayed, smoky tone in the pupils. Otherwise he was not a bad-looking guy.

A kid like Abigail, I thought, the way things are nowadays, could get carried away by the idea of a big-little operator like Caccelli—a guy neither hip nor square, far enough out from Main Street to be interesting but not freaky enough to be dangerous.

"Lately?" I prompted him.

"I think he's screwing me," Caccelli said. "I want to check him out."

"You mean you want me to check him out?"

"Yeah. Go to San Diego, check out the operation."

He pulled a wallet from his jacket pocket, opened it, took out a bill and dropped it on the coffee table. It was a thousand-dollar bill.

"Traveling money," he said. "I'll treat you right."

I let the bill lie there.

"I don't know—" I said. "You must have guys on your payroll who know a lot more about the operation than I could learn in six months."

"I got some watchdogs," he said, "but they're busy around here. I can't spare them."

"I really don't know much about the vending machine business. I don't know whether I could tell if Goldblatt is screwing you."

"You can count, can't you?"

"Anyway to a hundred," I said. "But—"

"You got something else going right now?"

"Well—no," I said. "I thought I had, but it didn't work out. But this kind of business—it's not my thing. Also I don't know anything about San Diego."

"There's nothing to know about San Diego. It's a place. Like all places."

"It's a place I've never been."

"Goldblatt is staying at the El Cortez," he said. "Room ten-thirteen. You can tell him I sent you down to help him out."

"That seems pretty transparent," I said. "If he's such a hot shot, why would he need help?"

"I said he was a hell of a salesman. I didn't say he was sharp. In fact, he's stupid. Except that he can count all right."

"Even so—"

I pretended to look at the money and Caccelli stayed right with me.

"There's more," he said. "I'll take care of you all right."

Uh-huh, I was thinking. *Here's a grand in advance, boy. Get out of town.*

This ploy with the thousand-dollar payoff would have to be transparent, even to Caccelli. Maybe it didn't matter to him. Maybe he knew that I knew he wanted me out of town and this was his first try, the easiest. If it didn't work, he would come up with something else.

"I'll take a look at it," I said. "What was that hotel again?"

I got out a note pad and pencil and Caccelli said, "El Cortez—it's right downtown—room ten-thirteen."

I wrote it down. "Guy's name is Goldblatt?"

"Yeah. Sam Goldblatt."

I stuck the note pad in my pocket along with the pencil and got up.

"There are four flights a day to San Diego," Caccelli said. "You could get one at three thirty, if you want to get in early."

He's in a hurry, I thought.

"Okay," I said.

I started away from the table and he said, "You forgot the bill."

I shook my head. "Won't be necessary," I said. "I've got credit cards. I'll keep track of expenses."

Caccelli didn't like it, but he stayed cool. "It's your thing," he said. "Keep in touch."

"Sure," I said.

The house boy got to the door one step ahead of me. I let him open it.

"See you," I said, and Caccelli waved and turned away.

Outside, the sun was hot without any sweetness.

My answering service had a message that said please call Lieutenant Shapiro. I tried, but Shapiro wasn't in. I dialed San Diego, got the number of the El Cortez Hotel and placed a person-to-person call to Sam Goldblatt. As I had hoped, he wasn't in either. After a while I tried Shapiro again and he came on.

"Just wondering," he said, "have you found any more dead ones?"

"No," I said. "No, I haven't. However, Mr. Caccelli just hired me to undertake a project in San Diego."

"How do you mean it—hired?"

"Well, he said he would pay generously and I said I would look into it."

"Uh-huh. So you're on your way to San Diego."

"I didn't say that. I think I took care of it already, no sense in Caccelli spending a lot of useless money. There's this guy working for him in San Diego, opening up the territory, as Caccelli puts it, and Caccelli thinks the guy is screwing him, knocking down or something. And I should go down there and—this guy's name is Goldblatt, Sam Goldblatt—and I should check him out. So what I did, I just called down there and I said, 'Mr. Goldblatt, Mr. Caccelli thinks maybe you are screwing him, is that true?' and Goldblatt said, 'Hell no, it's not true. I wouldn't screw Joe Caccelli,' and I said, 'Okay, just checking,' and I think that should take care of that."

Shapiro didn't say anything right away. When he did speak, he didn't sound amused. "You feeling pretty light-hearted and like that, huh?"

"I feel all right. Mystified, but not depressed."

"If Caccelli wants to get you out of town, he'll keep trying things till he finds one that will work."

"Well, that's his hangup."

"Sure."

"I'll have to wing it, Lieutenant. I've consulted my astrologer, the fair Gilda—that is, I told her when I was born. I understand she's working on it."

"Then I guess you'll be all right."

"If the stars are right."

"Okay, Mac. By the way, how can I get in touch with Peter Rinaldi?"

"I don't know. Honest."

"All right for now."

"No missing persons report on Michele Armande?"

"Not yet."

"I'll keep my eyes open."

"Thanks," he said, and hung up.

I didn't feel good. Shapiro appeared to think I might actually have seen a corpse the night before. He might think that somebody else had seen it too. If the corpse had once housed the living personality Michele Armande, it might have been viewed by her husband, Peter Rinaldi. It might be that if Shapiro had two witnesses instead of only one, he could assume that a crime had been committed. Then he could get on it.

Why? I thought. He hasn't got enough?

Somebody knocked at the door.

"Come in," I said, trying to decide whether to push a few papers, look busy, or whether it would be all right to slump at my ease in the swivel chair behind my desk. It turned out that it wouldn't have mattered much either way.

A guy came in, guy about twenty-six, twenty-seven, dressed in blue jeans, black boots, blue denim shirt, corduroy jacket and hair down to his shoulder blades. The hair was stringy and the look around the eyes was what they call spacy—that is, freaky. It is a look that combines jollity with vacuity. You know that if it should laugh, it would resemble a wolf laughing. The thought of it sets my teeth on edge to this day.

He stood in his boots halfway between my desk and the door by which he had entered.

"You the private eye Mac?" he said.

"Maybe," I said. "Who are you?"

"Dig, man," he said. "I'll drive you to the airport. No charge, gratis."

"Drive me in what?" I said. "A tumbrel?"

He didn't know the word and he didn't like being confused. He frowned. If he had laughed, I think I would have thrown something at him.

"Thanks for the offer," I said, "but I'll make it on my own. I'm not ready to leave."

"I'll wait," he said. "Mr. Caccelli told me to take you to the airport."

"So take the day off," I said. "I know the way to the airport."

He made a karate chop gesture at the air, a slicing movement. It wasn't a threat, just something to do with his hands. His kind can't take much frustration. Mental frustration that is.

"I appreciate Mr. Caccelli's kindness," I said, "I really do. But I'm not ready to go and I have quite a lot to do. So if you will excuse me—"

I pushed some papers, and that was when he laughed. And it was like a wolf laughing. He came at the desk in his loud boots. I gave him three steps and pushed the desk at him very hard and fast over the linoleum. It hit him at about groin level and he came sliding across it, face down. I was on my feet then, and I hit him with both hands on the back of his neck. At the last second, not wanting to really kill him, I pulled the punch, and that was a mistake, a real beaut.

He growled in his throat and his right fist, moving like a pitched baseball with the momentum of his slide, slammed into the soft part of my diaphragm. I backed all the way to the wall on my heels, fighting for breath. He came on over the desk and twisted to get a foothold on the floor. I managed to reach him before he found his balance and hammered on his neck and then his lower ribs till he went down. He fell heavily and stopped moving. I was half-unconscious from loss of wind, but I remember being scared, thinking maybe I had killed him after all. I didn't bother to check on it, though, till after I got my breath back. I was very hot, both with rage and exertion, and I hated to touch him, but I made myself lift one of his eyelids and he was all right, just not moving.

The telephone had left the desk when I pushed it, and I could hear the signal buzzing stridently. It changed from the steady buzz to the busy signal as I picked it up and set it on the desk. I leaned against the desk and looked at him for a while. When he stirred, I prodded him with my foot till he made a sound.

"All right," I said, "just lie there and rest."

I picked up the phone and dialed Caccelli's home number. The brown boy answered and when I asked for Caccelli, he said he wasn't in. I asked where he was and the guy on the floor lifted his head and said, "Don't call Mr. Caccelli."

"Take it easy," I said.

The brown boy thought maybe Caccelli was in his office downtown. I thanked him and hung up.

"What's your name?" I asked the one on the floor.

He rolled onto his back and lay with his arms outflung and his feet splayed.

"Clyde," he said.

"You work for Caccelli on a regular basis?"

"No," he said, "just special jobs."

I was flattered.

I guess he took my conversational gambit as a friendly gesture, because he rolled over and started to get up.

"Don't get up," I said.

He tested me, holding his big frame on his braced hands.

"Believe me, I'll kick your head in," I said.

He lowered himself to a supine position and stared at the ceiling. His eyes didn't blink. I picked up the phone and started to dial Caccelli's office and the door opened behind me. I ducked as I looked around, but it was only the fair Gilda, in that lovely skirt, swirling, and no shoes and her golden hair swishing around her face and shoulders. When she caught sight of the guy on the floor she stopped dead, except that her hair kept on swinging.

"Am I interrupting something?" she said.

"No," I said. "Come right in. Hey, Clyde, what's your birthdate?"

72

He grunted something.

"When were you born?" I said.

"April," he said, "April 17."

Gilda smiled happily. "He's an Aries!" she said. "This is a good day for him. Why is he laying down?"

"He's lying down because he's a little under the weather," I said.

"I mean lying," she said. "Oh dear."

"Maybe you read the key wrong," I said.

"No, I'm positive," she said. "I remember the day very clearly because it's the same as Allie Quinn's date—she's an Aries too—and Allie never had a bad March 8 in her life. Allie is a schoolteacher and she's been promoted every year for four years and now she's the best paid teacher in her school and—"

"Good for Allie," I said. "When was Caccelli born, Clyde?"

He said a bad word and turned his face away from us.

"Oh dear," Gilda said, "he's very angry, isn't he?"

"I don't know," I said. "Keep your eye on him while I call his employer."

"Don't call Caccelli," Clyde said.

"Who else?" I said.

"Listen, don't call anybody. I'll be all right. I'll go. I won't put a hand on you."

"I'm sure of that," I said, "but where will you go?"

"I got a place to go."

"I want to make it clear to Mr. Caccelli that you're not to come back," I said.

"I won't come back."

"Even if Mr. Caccelli gives you twenty dollars?"

He didn't say anything.

Gilda came close and put her warm lips to my ear, causing it to tingle. "Your own key is not very good for this date," she whispered.

"I think I got that message," I said. "But thanks."

"I guess I'd better go," she said.

"If you must," I said, "but blow in my ear again and I'll come after you."

"Oh dear," she said, and skipped out of the room.

I hoped she wouldn't stay away too long. Her action was a lot more attractive than Clyde's.

Clyde—?

I dialed Caccelli's office number and a brisk, secretarial voice identified "Star-Line Enterprises." I asked for Caccelli and she said he wasn't in.

"Will he be back?" I asked.

"Not today. He's out of town."

"Oh. He must have gone to San Diego."

"No—I mean, I don't know where he went."

But not to San Diego, I thought.

I thanked her and hung up.

"Well, Clyde," I said, "I guess you'd better split. I can't think of anything to do about you. Just don't come back."

He took his time getting on his feet. He didn't feel quite well, but then again he could move around all right, once he stirred himself. He gave me plenty of clearance and I watched him across the room and out the door. He was not a pleasant sight. He would be back in one way or another, if not in this room, then somewhere around the corner, probably after dark. He would get to me if he could. And no doubt he could. You can't lose them for sure without killing them.

Meanwhile, I decided, there was little to be done about the case of Michele Armande. My real assignment

74

was to protect Peter Rinaldi from abuse, and I couldn't do that without his cooperation.

Interesting, I thought—you can't force a man to live if he's otherwise inclined.

I put the desk back where it belonged, left the office, making sure the door was locked, and went by the back stairs to the second floor, to the digs of Gilda the astrologer. Her door was open and she was alone with her astrolabe and a sheaf of blank paper. I went in and sat down on a love seat facing her desk, and I was there for at least three minutes before she became aware of my presence. She jumped half out of her chair and put her hand to her throat.

"Oh dear," she said, "you ought not to sneak up on a body that way."

"On a body?" I said.

"Just an expression."

"I guess I'm hypersensitive."

"You are sensitive, you know," she said. "Your readings all indicate great sensitivity. For that reason, during these few days, you should especially avoid emotional stress."

"I don't have emotional stress," I said. "Just physical."

"You mean like that strange man in your office?"

"I guess that's what I mean. How would you like to have lunch with me and discuss my—key."

"Oh I'm so sorry. I can't today, I have an appointment —in fact in about five minutes from now."

"I'm having emotional stress now," I said "Another time, okay?"

"Yes, by all means."

"So long for now."

"So long, Mac."

I felt lonely. She was a cute chick. What did I care if she was ape for astrology? So was Chaucer, and a lot of cats before and after.

Taurus ascending, I thought, going on down the stairs to the street level. Ruled by Venus. Think of a notable born under Taurus, ruled by Venus.

I couldn't think of any notables at all, let alone Taurus ruled by Venus. I liked the idea of being ruled by Venus, but Venus Gilda had been unable to accommodate me. I reminded myself to pin her down about my key and try to learn what to expect.

Heading for the parking area behind the building, I stepped into the alley, stepped back hard against the already closed door and sucked in my stomach as a panel truck swerved toward me, passed and stopped twenty feet to my right toward the cross street. The truck was unlabeled, was dusty as if it had traveled a long distance, and smelled hot. The back door opened and a guy fell —or was pushed—out onto the blacktop. The doors closed and the panel truck pulled away fast. The guy was lying in the middle of the alley, his head in his folded arms. He moved, but he didn't get up. It was Peter Rinaldi.

7

WHEN I got to him, he had rolled onto his side and was trying to get up. There was some blood on his face, though not much, and his suit jacket was torn at one shoulder. He had been hit hard under the left eye and seemed to have difficulty opening it. He jumped when I touched him.

"It's all right," I said. "It's me, Mac. What happened?"

"Those . . . same two," he said.

"All right, let me help you inside. We can talk later."

I got my hands under his arms and raised him to his feet. He was shaky and very unsteady, but he walked all right with my help. I got the back door open and held it with my shoulders while I eased him inside. Gilda came skipping down the stairs, dressed to go out. There was a guy behind her, not skipping. I decided I didn't like him.

Rinaldi and I couldn't get anywhere until they cleared the rear passage. Gilda took a look at Rinaldi and then at me.

"Oh dear," she said, "another one. When was he born?"

"On a bad day," I said. "Excuse us."

Her escort was out of the way, and the two of them went out as I led Rinaldi to the steps and made him sit down. He sat with his head in his hands.

"You didn't get very far after you left here, huh?"

"I was driving home," he said. "They forced me off the road about halfway up the canyon. I guess the car's still there. . . . I don't . . ."

He started to fall forward and I caught him and hung onto him.

"Get you to a hospital," I said.

"No, I'll be all right . . ."

"What did they want from you?"

"They said, . . . 'Stay away' . . . they said, 'Stay away from the private eye.' "

"Meaning me?"

"Who else?"

"Then they brought you back here and dumped you on my doorstep."

"I guess . . . they did, yes."

"Can you make it over to my car?"

"I think so."

"Let's go."

I gave him some support and we got outside and across to the parking lot. I opened the car door and put him in the front seat, went around and got under the wheel. The nearest hospital was on Alvarado near Sunset and it would take a few minutes.

"You better take me to my car," he said, "I'll be all right . . . I could lie down . . ."

"You can lie down in the hospital," I said. "I want you in a safe place so I don't have to go around picking you up all the time."

"Sorry . . ."

"Just relax," I said. "Talk if you feel like it. But don't push it."

He didn't say anything till I was squared away on Sunset, heading for Alvarado toward downtown Los Angeles.

"They are the same two," he said, "that came to Michele's apartment last night. But I don't know who they are."

"Are they still in the movie business?" I asked.

"What—I don't follow you."

"You said, the first time you saw them they wanted to talk to you about a picture deal."

"That's right."

So he was clamming again. We had been through it all before. The hell with it.

"I'll go see about your car as soon as I get you checked in," I said. "Don't worry about it."

"I really think—"

"Mr. Rinaldi," I said, "I don't want to be rude, but the evidence seems to show that this is not the most auspicious time for you to try thinking. Your key indicates that it would be best to lay off thinking altogether for about eight days. By the way, when *were* you born?"

"When was I—? Please—"

"I'm not asking your age, just the day of the month."

"Oh . . . September ninth . . . or tenth . . . there's some confusion in the records."

I had no idea what his sign was anyway, so I let it go.

"You dabble in astrology too?" he said.

I didn't like that one. Dabble. The hell with dabble.

"No," I said, "but I have friends."

"I see."

I see again! Rinaldi, I thought, if you can get Mary Dane to fire me, I'll accept it with good grace.

I got to the hospital, and after I had waited a few minutes and had given them a hundred dollars in cash, they sent a couple of orderlies out to the car and put Rinaldi on a stretcher.

"Will you . . . ," he said, "please call Mary."

"Yes," I said, "and I'll see that your car gets home. You stay here. If you decide to leave, be sure and call me first. And don't leave unless I say so."

"I can't afford this—" he said.

"I'll work that out," I said. "Take it easy now."

It was a thin goodbye, but he would be safe for a while and off my Taurus mind.

You get off in those canyons and you feel as if you were back on the old frontier. Every structure is something that was hacked out of the surrounding brush, and then everybody went away and left it. Nobody ever seems to be living in them. Every once in a while beside the road there will be a hacked-out spot big enough to put a car in, sometimes big enough to turn a truck around in. The rest is brush and rock. It was in one of these I found Peter Rinaldi's car, a Ford product about three years old. It was white—or, by now, gray-white, and in good condition except for a twist in the bumper on the right.

It had been pulled in close to the cut on its left. There was space beside it for another car and that was about all. I guessed the panel truck could have pulled in there too. They would have been crowding him for some time up the hill and finally he would have turned into the cut, hoping they would get off of him.

Why had they dumped him at my back door?

Because, I guessed, it was a way of bugging me, the way they had bugged him up that canyon road.

But what did they want from me?

I pulled clear of the road, got out of the car and walked to Rinaldi's Ford. The door was not locked and I leaned in and took a first look. There wasn't much litter, a few match covers on the floor, an umbrella on the back seat, yesterday's newspaper folded on the far side of the front seat. The ignition keys were still in the slot and I put them in my pocket. I tried the glove compartment and it was locked. I got out the keys, unlocked it and pulled out what was in it: two road maps, one of California, Arizona and Nevada and one of Los Angeles County; a couple of parking tickets, an Auto Club card, some blue chip stamps, and an envelope addressed to Mr. Peter Rinaldi at Mary Dane's address. I held the envelope up to the light and saw there was something inside it. I put it in my pocket along with the car keys.

I felt around under the front seat, found nothing, opened the left rear door and got in there and pulled the back of the rear seat forward. There was some trash behind it, more match covers, clots of congealed dust, scraps of paper. I looked at several of the scraps, and nothing was written on any of them. There was an abandoned ballpoint pen and a snapshot of an unidentified baby of about three months. I looked on the back and saw that it was a sample submission to a Hollywood casting directory. The name of the baby was Will Provence.

I could find nothing on the floor of the back seat, and

I got out and opened the trunk. It was the neatest compartment of the car. It contained a spare tire, snugly bolted down, a bag of tools, a bumper jack and an empty orange crate. I was raising my right hand to lower the trunk top when a dusty panel truck pulled in close at the edge of the cut, effectively blocking exit by either Rinaldi's car or mine. There were two guys in the front seat. They were both known to me by sight.

I reached with one hand, feeling for the bag of tools. One of them was one of those old-fashioned, L-shape lug wrenches. The two of them came out of the truck as I got my hand on the wrench. But they had only three and a half feet of space to cover and one of them had a gun. It was trained on me and out of reach and they didn't care about my lug wrench.

The one with the gun stood off and the other one came on fast, eased the wrench from my hand and turned me around, facing into the trunk.

"Just lean there easy," he said.

It was the one with the tight voice and the skin graft. It occurred to me that the other one had abandoned his shades somewhere.

I leaned there, reminding myself to watch out for the trunk lid, so as not to bump my head in case I should get a chance to emerge. His hands banged at me lightly, pockets above, pockets below. He found the envelope and keys in my jacket pocket and pulled them out. He felt my wallet in my inside jacket pocket and left it alone. I had no weapons on me. In one of my hip pockets I had a handkerchief and in the other a thin black notebook about two by three inches. It was of importance only to me. He pulled that out and failed to return it. I edged my right hand over the handle of the lug wrench and waited.

"Listen—" the guy said.

I started to turn my head and he gave it a hard push.

"Stay there, just listen," he said. "You're messing around with stuff that don't concern you. There's no skin off you—yet. But you can lose skin if you keep messing with it. So pull out."

"I dig," I said. "Okay."

"Okay," he said. "Just hang in the trunk there till we're gone."

"Sure," I said. "I'm not going anywhere."

I was thinking about it. The one talking to me had come out first. He had not been the driver. The driver was the one with the gun. He would either have to get in first, or wait for the other to get in, then go around the car and climb under the wheel. He wouldn't do that. He would get in first and either hand the gun to the other one, or take a small chance and drop the gun on the seat. In any case, there would be a few seconds in which neither of them would be in a position to make much trouble.

A few seconds is not long. I could hear the footsteps on the gravel of the cut, and then the squeaking lurch of the truck springs as one of them got into the seat. It seemed forever before the second one sounded the squeak; it was probably a second and a half. The best break I had was that their engine had stalled.

The slam of the door was simultaneous with the rattle of the starter. I had a good grip on the wrench when I backed from the trunk, turning to find them. I bumped my head on the lid but all I felt was the impact, no pain.

The driver was shoving into low gear when I let fly. The wrench smashed hard against the near window. It was shatterproof and the sunburst of radiating cracks covered it completely. Among the cracks I could see the rider duck down. Then the door opened and he came out. I was waiting for him.

He had the car door to cope with, small room to move in, and I got him with both hands on either side of the soft places below his ribs. He swung on me with his right hand, but there was no force in it and I kept the squeeze on him. He was between me and the one with the gun and that was good for the moment, but there was a lot to be done. He jabbed me in the neck. It hurt. I let him come forward a little and when he relaxed I shoved him back and upward and banged the back of his head against the door frame. He was breathing in gasps because his wind was shut off, the way I was holding him. I couldn't see the other one, but I felt the truck lurch and knew he was getting out on the other side. I banged the guy's head again and he slumped down against me. I dragged him clear of the truck and turned, holding him up as a shield as the other one came around the front end. The one I was holding was heavy as hell, and I knew I couldn't keep him up long. I tightened the grip on his soft flesh and he made a bad sound.

"The way I've got him," I said to the other one, "he'll strangle to death if I don't let up. Drop the gun."

I gave a hard squeeze and the guy screamed. I guess that's what did it. I saw the gun fall, off to my right. I let go of the heavy one and he flopped at my feet, hugging his sides with his elbows. My arms were pumping blood into my hands like they were on fire. The other one took a step and I braced him.

"Go ahead, go for it," I said. "See what happens."

He eyed the gun and the one on the ground, and he didn't go for it. The thing was halfway between us plus a step right for me, left for him. I had the advantage. I don't know whether he realized it or not, but he didn't make a move when I stepped over and picked it up.

"Get back in the truck," I said.

He hesitated, but not for long. He went around the front end to the driver's side and climbed in. The one on the ground was on his hands and knees. I put my thumb on the hammer of the gun and flashed it at him.

"Give me the stuff you got from my pockets," I said.

He raised himself, dug into his jacket pocket and came up with the envelope and the car keys.

"The notebook," I said.

He went to the other pocket and brought out the notebook. The items made a scraggly pile on the gravel. He was still on his knees and I could practically feel the rough gravel biting into them. I thumbed the hammer again.

"What's your name?" I asked him.

He stared at me.

"My hand tends to shake," I said. "What's your name?"

"Riordan," he said. "Chick Riordan."

"What's the other one's name?"

"Dennis. Morrie Dennis."

I looked through the door frame at the driver. "Morrie," I said, "who sent you?"

"The boss," he said.

"Jack Boss?"

He shrugged.

"Caccelli?" I said.

He didn't say anything. I looked at the other one, Riordan, and decided I had neither the time nor the leverage to get a lot of information out of them. The chances of its being useful were negligible anyway. I hadn't enough to go on to make an evaluation. They hadn't denied Caccelli, but they hadn't confirmed him either. It looked like Caccelli though.

"All right," I said, "this is what we're going to do. Chick here will drive Rinaldi's car up the road to Mary Dane's house. Morrie will follow in the truck. I will follow the two of you. At Mary Dane's house, Morrie will turn the truck around and Chick will get in it. You will drive on down the road to wherever you have to go. Got that?"

It wasn't so awfully chancy. They would do it, eight to two. In that canyon, one well-placed slug could spin them into eternity. They had to think about it. They couldn't run away from me because it was uphill and they could tell at a glance that my car would overtake both Rinaldi's Ford and their truck.

Riordan got stiffly to his feet, pulling gingerly at his pants to unglue them from his bloody knees.

"Pick up the keys and get in Rinaldi's car," I said.

He picked them up and went over there. I pushed the truck door shut and motioned to the driver to back away. He got it started and backed. I stopped him. I went to Rinaldi's Ford and Riordan was under the wheel.

"You know where the house is," I said. "Drive about twenty miles an hour. Leave the car outside the front gate."

I waited while he started it.

"Go ahead," I said, "keep it moving, slow."

He backed onto the street in front of the truck and squared it away heading uphill. I was in my own car, backing, as the truck moved ahead following the Ford.

When I got onto the road, we were about forty feet apart. I closed the gap to twenty. The gun was on the seat beside me, along with the envelope I had found in Rinaldi's glove compartment. I had plenty of time to memorize the license number of the truck: NCA 487.

The pace picked up when we hit Dead Man's Curve, but it wasn't what you would call breathtaking, and after he negotiated the curve, Riordan eased onto the Dane drive at the big gate and came to a stop, like an obedient Irishman should. Dennis went on up the road out of sight, but when I swung in behind Riordan, Dennis had made his turn and was drifting back to the drive.

"Okay," I said to Riordan, "get out and into the truck."

He got out and walked over to the truck, eyeing the gun, which I stuck in my pocket.

"You can claim it at my office," I said, "Monday to Friday, eight to four."

He got in the truck, slammed the door and they started down the hill. When they were out of sight, I withdrew the contents of Rinaldi's envelope and leaned against the fender of my car, reading it. The light was none too good, what with the hazy sky and the trees all around, but I could make out the words, written in a scrawly, barely legible hand.

"Dear Peter: This is from your devoted wife Michele. I guess you thought I was dead. So did a lot of people. But I don't want to play dead anymore and I need to see you. Don't let me down or I'll blow my little whistle. Lovingly, Michele."

A sweet kid, I thought.

A less pleasant thought was running through my head. If she really had a Rinaldi tune in her whistle, and if she was tired of make-believe death—whatever that was

—maybe Rinaldi had fixed it by making it real for her. Similar domestic tragedies have been known to occur.

I heard a squeaking sound. The gate moved a few inches on one side, opening. A woman said, "Hello—? Who's there, please?"

"Miss Dane," I said, "it's me, Mac."

"Oh. Are you coming in?"

"In a minute," I said.

I couldn't see her. I put Rinaldi's letter in my inside pocket and went to the gate. She was standing just inside it, peering out through the four-inch opening she had made. She looked fragile as old China and prettier than she had any right to look at her age. Mary Dane, princess of the silver screen.

8

THE GATE was heavy and the hinges ground in a kind of agony as I pushed it open. Mary Dane looked at the two cars and said nothing.

"Peter," I said, "is in the hospital. He's going to be all right, but I'd like him to stay there a while."

"He was injured?"

"In a way," I said. "I've brought his car back. He can get home from the hospital in a taxi."

"Yes," she said.

She was looking at the two cars, first at one and then the other.

"You're quite remarkable," she said. "Two cars at once—"

"I had some help," I said.

"I'm glad of that."

"I'll just ease Peter's car inside the gate, all right?"

"Of course."

I went to Rinaldi's car. The gun was a bad load in my pocket, and without thinking I pulled it out and tossed it onto the seat. Then I saw that Mary Dane was watching.

"Excuse me," I said, "the help I had needed encouragement."

"I see," she said.

It seemed all right, coming from her. When Rinaldi said it, it was a bad phrase.

She stood well out of the way as I drove into the carport among the well-kept trees. I left the car and brought the keys to her, and she held them in one fragile hand in an unaccustomed way.

"You may be uneasy, being alone in the house," I said. "Would you like me to arrange for someone to come in for a few days?"

"Oh, no, I'll be fine," she said. "If I need anything, Abigail can get it for me. But how long will Peter have to stay in the hospital? Is he badly hurt?"

"No, not badly," I said, "but he needs a rest. He ought to stay a couple of days, I think. He's worried about the cost."

"He needn't."

"That's what I thought. I gave the hospital a hundred."

"Include it in your charges to me," she said.

"All right."

She laid those clear, bright eyes on me. "Peter is in serious trouble, isn't he?"

"He may be," I said. "I'm not sure. From an official viewpoint—police, that is—what I saw with my own eyes was not true. I'm not sure I saw it. I'm not sure Peter had anything to do with it."

"What was it you saw?"

"A dead woman," I said, "a Michele Armande."

"Michele—? No!"

"That was my understanding. Mrs. Peter Rinaldi."

"You know about that?"

"Yes."

There was a short period of silence.

"Maybe I don't know enough about it," I said.

She looked away toward the brush-covered hills. "I couldn't say," she said. "It's Peter's story. I think he'll tell you when the time comes."

"No doubt," I said. "I guess I'd better be getting on with it. I'll keep in touch."

"Yes, thank you for everything—for taking care of Peter."

"I'll do my best, ma'am."

"Goodbye," she said.

I nodded, remembered the gun and went to Rinaldi's car to get it. She watched me put it in my pocket and said nothing. She didn't say anything as I passed her on the way out. I offered to close the gate for her and she declined the offer. She said Abigail would be coming soon and it might as well be left open.

Abigail's red Jaguar was tearing around the deadly curve on the wrong side of the road as I started down. I pulled up short, as far over as I could get, and she saw me in time to swerve past without making contact. I felt the breeze, though.

When she was in the clear I went on down the canyon, watching for panel trucks along the way. By the time I got to Sunset Boulevard I had decided that Chick Riordan and Morrie Dennis had had enough for that day. They would be back, though. There were three of them I could expect now—those two and Clyde. I took the gun out of my pocket and laid it on the seat.

If I get stopped for anything, such as a defective curb finder, I told myself, I wouldn't want the lads to find me with the gun in my pocket.

Some rationalization.

I put the car in my parking slot and was crossing the alley to the back door when a black and white patrol car swung in from the cross street. No sooner did one, or both, of the cops set eyes on me than the red light started flashing. I stopped. The rider officer got out, unbuckling his holster as he came. I held the gun out in plain sight, pointing at the pavement. He came to within six feet of me and he was slapping leather.

"The gun yours?" he said.

"No," I said.

"Where are you going with it?"

"Up to my office."

"Where did the gun come from?"

"I took it off a guy, about an hour ago."

"You plan to turn it in?"

"Sure. I was about to call Lieutenant Shapiro."

"Lay the gun down on the street," he said, "and show me an ID. We'll call Shapiro."

I stooped carefully, far enough to lay the piece down, then straightened up. I hope Shapiro is in, I thought.

I pulled out my wallet and flashed my driver's license and my PI card.

"Take them out of the wallet," he said.

I slipped them out and handed them over. He beckoned and his partner came up behind him.

"Call Shapiro in homicide," he said. "Check out a PI—Mac—"

He showed him the card. The other officer took it and went back to the car. I stood and waited.

"Who did you take it from?" the cop asked.

"Guy named Morrie Dennis."

"How come?"

"He was pointing it at me."

92

"Did you shoot him?"

"No, no need for that."

The other cop returned. "Lieutenant Shapiro says to put him on," he said.

I walked between them to the patrol car, and the one officer picked off the speaking gadget and handed it to me. The Lieutenant's voice came scratchy over the car radio.

"Mac, what the hell are you into?"

"I don't know. A couple of guys braced me up in Brenthill Canyon. One of them had a gun and I took it away from him and was heading for the office.

"Who were the guys?"

I told him.

"All right, put the officer on."

"What about the gun?" I said.

"Turn it over to him."

"I told the guys they could claim it at my office."

"Tell 'em the cops took it away from you."

"All right."

I handed the mike to the officer and heard the Lieutenant tell him to take over the gun, give me a receipt and let loose of me. The cop said, "Yes, sir."

The second officer went to the gun, picked it up, checked the safety and the load and brought it to the car. The other was writing out a receipt for me. I signed it and they nodded a little stiffly and got in their car and drove away.

As Lieutenant Donovan had told me in Chicago, "They've got a lot of organization in Los Angeles."

I went into the building and headed up the stairs to the office. I was midway between the second floor and my penthouse when Gilda came skipping out of her office and

93

up the stairs behind me. I went on to the top and she stood around while I unlocked the office door.

"What did they want?" she asked breathlessly.

"Who?"

"The police down there."

"They wanted to know what I was doing with a gun in my hand."

"Oh dear," she said.

I got the door open and she went swirling in ahead of me.

"Well," I said, "you tried to warn me. What was in my key for today? You never actually told me."

"I didn't think you'd take it seriously."

"I take everything you say seriously."

"Don't put me on."

"Never."

"Well—your key for today says this: Unpredictable: gambles of a monetary or emotional nature are just as apt to turn against you as for you. Down-to-earth methods are much surer."

"Down-to-earth methods," I said. "You don't say. And I did gamble on taking you to lunch, and I lost, didn't I?"

"Have you lost any money yet?"

"Can't say I lost it, but I did spend quite a chunk unexpectedly."

She nodded wisely.

"What about that character, that freak on the floor?" I asked. "What's his key?"

"Let's see . . . he was an Aries . . ."

"That's right."

"It was a good day for him."

"Not altogether."

"His key says: Jobs that are annoying can be turned into unmitigated pleasure through the use of originality. It's the attitude that really counts."

"Amazing," I said.

"What do you mean by that?" She was suspicious.

"You remember all these—every day, for every birth-date?"

"Of course not. But I do have a good memory, especially for words, and I looked yours up again a few minutes ago."

"Did you look up Clyde's?"

"Clyde—? Oh, that freak? No. But I told you, that's the same date as Allie Quinn's. Allie's my best—"

"Yes, I remember about Allie."

The telephone rang. I turned to pick it up and Gilda let out a yelp.

"Hey—!"

"Yeah?" I said.

"Mac—your head's all bloody!"

I put my hand to the back of my head and, sure enough, I could feel the blood, crusted by now in my hair and on my neck. I remembered bumping it on the lid of the car trunk.

"Yeah," I said, and picked up the phone.

Lieutenant Shapiro was on the other end. Gilda ran out of the room. I decided she was going to be sick at the sight of my blood. Shapiro was saying, "Those two you had a ruckus with—Riordan and Dennis?"

"Yes," I said.

"Are they the two you saw at the hypothetical murder scene last night?"

Suddenly I was fed up with the make-believe.

"Hypothetical hell!" I said. "There was a dead body. I saw it, felt it. It disappeared."

"All right," he said patiently. "But were these guys the ones you saw?"

"Yeah."

Gilda danced back into the office with a wet towel in one hand and a dry one in the other. She was very gentle and nice. The towel was warm and soothing on the back of my head.

"I've got a pickup order out for them," Shapiro said, "If we bring them in, will you come down and identify them, sign a complaint?"

"What kind of a complaint?"

"Well, if you had to take the gun off of them—didn't they put up any kind of a fight at all?"

Gilda touched a sore spot and I winced.

"Uh—yes, yes they did," I said.

"Then you can make a complaint, so I can book them."

"I'll do it if you'll let me ask them some questions of my own," I said.

"Whatever's fair," he said.

"Let me know when."

"One more thing, Mac. Where's Peter Rinaldi?"

"He's in the hospital."

"Serious?"

"No, for safekeeping."

"Same two fellows?"

"Riordan and Dennis—yeah."

"Okay, take it easy."

"Sure."

I hung up. Gilda had finished cleaning my wound and was dabbing at it with the dry towel.

"It's not going to bleed anymore," she said.

"I'm glad. Blood is messy."

"How did it happen?"

"I bumped my head on the lid of the trunk—the car trunk."

"Oh dear," she said, disappointed. "Is that all?"

"I'll try to make it more glamorous the next time."

"I wondered—because of the police and all—"

"That was another matter."

"Oh," she said.

I put my arm around her and gave her a hug. "Look, baby," I said, "there's no big secret or anything and I'll tell you all about it as soon as I get a chance, but right now I've got some work to do, all right?"

"All right, I'll leave you alone."

"I don't mean you have to leave me alone. I just have to look into a couple of things."

"I know. I'll go back to work too."

"Will you cast me a horoscope for the next few days? Regular rates?"

"No rates for you," she said. "I'll have it for you in an hour."

I released her and she skipped away, her short skirt flapping happily around her good thighs.

I opened the middle drawer of my desk and found the notes I'd made on the scene of Michele Armande's hanging.

Hypothetical, my fanny! I thought.

The notes were skimpy. I had done a brief report to myself on what I had found around the apartment and on the condition of the body. The only tangible piece of a lead had been that postcard from a place called North Pine, with its picture of North Pine Lodge. Peter Rinaldi's midnight message had said that Michele Armande had died eight or nine years ago, somewhere up north.

I got out my California map and finally found North Pine. It was in the vicinity of Mount Whitney in the Sierras. I had never been in those parts. I could assume that Michele Armande had been there at one time or another.

I called the Auto Club and got someone in the travel service department. I asked for a rundown on North Pine Lodge, and the lady promised to call back right away. I looked through the notes again, found nothing to take off from, and was pondering the dull ache in the back of my head when the Auto Club lady called.

"That's a small fishing and hunting resort, rustic style," she said. "It used to be quite fashionable and exclusive, I understand, but not anymore. You can probably get a reservation easily."

"To go fishing, for instance?" I asked.

"Well . . . not this time of year. I think it's the hunting season now—just a minute . . . yes, the season opens tomorrow. It's quite short. Come to think of it, it might be a little late for a reservation."

"I'm not sure I want to go, but thanks," I said.

"You're quite welcome."

She hung up.

"The hunting season," I said to myself.

Gilda skipped in with a sheet of paper in her hand.

"Ready?" she said.

"Lay it on," I said.

"During the next week," she said, "you ought to get out

and mingle more. Don't withdraw into yourself and brood. That's negative. Various people are involved in the problems you're having, and they seem like big problems at the moment. But you can't solve them by playing hermit."

She paused and then went on with as mischievous a smile as it has ever been my pleasure to see on such a face as hers.

"Remember—you're Taurus, ascendant now, ruled by Venus. Everyone needs love and companionship. If you bear that in mind, you'll be able to do the things necessary to bring peace and harmony into your life."

"Come here," I said.

After a second she put one finger in her mouth and came close enough for me to reach her.

"Will you have dinner with me?" I asked.

"Tonight?"

"Tonight, in about half an hour."

"Isn't that a little early?"

"Not by the time we have half a dozen drinks."

"I can't drink all that much."

"Okay, you can watch me drink."

"Do you drink a lot?"

"Hardly at all, except when I'm celebrating."

"What are you celebrating tonight?"

"The peace and harmony I'm about to bring into my life."

She giggled. I gave her a kiss on the cheek and when she turned around, a pat on the behind. She skipped out of the office.

"I'll be down in half an hour," I said.

"All right."

9

I TOOK her to a small French restaurant in the vicinity of the hospital. It was sneaky but practical. I would have to see Rinaldi, and visiting hours started at eight. I would figure out what to do about Gilda when the time came.

She had a couple of drinks, got giggly and said "Oh dear" a lot. She was cute. She didn't want to talk about astrology, she said, because she didn't talk shop when she was eating. I thought it was a joke and almost laughed, but she was serious. She ordered chicken grand-mère and we had some champagne.

"Peace," I said.

"Harmony."

The champagne brought on more giggles, and by seven thirty she was sleepy.

"Oh dear," she said, "I hate to be such a pooper—"

"Don't apologize," I said. "The fact is, I have to make a call."

"Telephone?"

"No. I've got to visit a sick friend. I was going to suggest that we might continue later in the evening, if you'd like to."

It was a safe offer. She wasn't going to be waking up for later in the evening.

"You're sweet and thoughtful," she said.

"I try."

"You work long hours, don't you?" she said.

"Not always. I work when there's something to be done. Days can go by when there's nothing to do but sit and swat flies."

"There aren't any flies in California."

"All right."

She giggled and I paid the tab and we got out of there. Her apartment was in the Wilshire district, near Crenshaw, and I saw her inside and managed to get back to the hospital at five after eight. When I inquired after Peter Rinaldi at the front desk, a girl told me he had left.

"What time?" I asked.

She consulted a chart and said he had left in a taxi at seven fifteen.

"Did he leave a balance due?" I asked.

"No, his bill is paid—seventy-nine eighty-one."

So he had something left over for cab fare.

"Was he in good condition?" I asked.

"He was—ambulatory."

"Well—thanks," I said.

I found a telephone booth near the front entrance and dialed Mary Dane's number. A woman came on.

"Miss Dane?"

"No, this is Abigail," she said.

"Hi, Abby," I said, "this is Mac."

"Mac who?"

"Mac the detective."

"Oh," she said.

"I thought I might talk to Peter."

"He's not here."

She was pretty cool. I decided not to push her. "Okay, thanks," I said.

"You're welcome," she said.

What came between Abigail and me? I wondered. "Caccelli?" I said aloud.

Somebody sitting on a bench said, "What did you say?"

"Nothing," I said.

I went back to the desk and asked the lady, "Were you on duty when Mr. Rinaldi left?"

"Yes, I was."

"You remember him?"

"Yes. I remembered seeing him in the movies."

"Did he leave by himself?"

"No, there was a gentleman—someone waiting for him. They went out together."

"Do you remember what this guy looked like?"

"Not really. I was busy. There wasn't anything special about him."

"Can you tell me this: did Mr. Rinaldi make any telephone calls . . . from his room?"

"I wouldn't know."

"It would show up on his bill, wouldn't it?"

"You'd have to see the cashier about that."

I went to the cashier's window and asked if I could see Peter Rinaldi's bill. The cashier said I couldn't. I headed for the door and bumped into Lieutenant Shapiro, letting himself in from the street.

"Rinaldi?" Shapiro said.

"He split," I said. "Seven fifteen, with a guy. I don't know who. I don't know where he is."

Shapiro looked mournful. "I'd better have him picked up," he said.

"Why?"

"I want to talk to him, about his wife."

We went outside and leaned against Shapiro's car.

"How about Riordan and Dennis?" I asked.

"Nothing. They probably hit the border. We've got bad records on them. Riordan is still on parole, so I could get him for violation."

"Do they run errands for Caccelli?"

He gave me a longish look. "Why do you ask?"

"Just a hunch. Why was Caccelli in that beer joint last night?"

"Go ahead," Shapiro said, "keep guessing."

"It's your turn, Lieutenant."

"Yeah," he said, "they work for Caccelli. Muscle work."

"How about talking to Caccelli?"

"In due time," Shapiro said, "in due time."

"You need a handle on Caccelli?"

"Yup."

I told him about Clyde the freak.

"You've been busy, haven't you?" he said. "Clyde who?"

"I don't know his last name. I know he's an Aries, and this was supposed to be a good day for him."

Lou Shapiro gave me a funny look. "You ought to get more sleep," he said.

"I guess so. Keep your eyes open."

"Uh-huh," he said.

I left him leaning against his car and found my own in the hospital parking lot. I pulled out of there, drove aimlessly for a while and stopped at a streetside phone. I dialed Mary Dane's number again, and this time got Miss Dane.

"Peter hasn't come home," she said. "I thought he planned to stay in the hospital."

"That was my plan," I said. "I guess Peter had ideas of his own."

"Where do you suppose he could be?"

"I wish I knew, Miss Dane. Is Abigail still with you?"

"No, her husband came for her and they left a few minutes ago."

"Are you all right?"

"I'm fine, but I'm worried about Peter."

"Try not to worry. I'll find him."

Big words, soothing words.

"I hope so," she said.

I said good-bye and hung up. I had no more idea than Mary Dane had where to look for Rinaldi. I got back in the car and drove about a block and a half, pulled over to the curb and turned on my think machine. It ran slug-gishly.

Champagne, I thought.

With what person would Rinaldi willingly leave the hospital?

His lawyer.

There are thousands of lawyers in Los Angeles.

Caccelli?

But it probably hadn't been Caccelli because the girl at the desk had said there was nothing special about him. Caccelli was special—a shorty. She would remember a short guy.

Fogel, I thought. Ed Fogel, who had befriended Rinaldi in the past.

If Rinaldi made a call from the hospital, if he wanted out, it would probably be Fogel he would call.

I could call Fogel myself. If I could find his telephone number.

I went to another phone booth and looked through the available directories covering the central and western sections of the city. There were about twenty-five E. Fogel, Ed Fogel, Edw. Fogel entries, and I picked out those with addresses in Beverly Hills, Brentwood and on such streets as Roscomare, Chalon Road, Bellagio, etc., and that brought the possibilities down to about five. I called all of them, got two no-answers, and talked to three. None of the three was the director Ed Fogel.

I called Mary Dane, as I should have done in the first place and she said of course she knew Ed Fogel's number. She gave me his residence number, then his office number. I wrote them down. I thanked her and said some reassuring words and hung up. With unusual care I dialed Fogel's residence. A woman came on and said Mr. Fogel wasn't home, she didn't know when to expect him, and she didn't know where he might be at the moment. I tried his office number and got an answering service and that was no help. I left no message.

I leaned heavily against the wall of the booth, wishing I were in the office with my necktie down and my feet up. I felt through my pockets and found the message Rinaldi had sent me the night before. "Michele Armande died eight or nine years ago, somewhere up north."

I looked up the number of the *L. A. Times,* dialed and asked if I could look at their back files.

"Not at this hour of the night," a woman said. "We have a library, open on Fridays by appointment."

"No way tonight?"

"Not unless you're an employee of the *Times.*"

"Well—" I said.

"The UCLA library has a complete file," she said. "I think they're open till midnight."

I thanked her and hung up. UCLA was a good twenty-five-minute drive from where I stood, but it would be a place to go, a thing to do.

The UCLA Research Library is no venerable, ivy-covered retreat, but a businesslike steel and concrete structure complete with elevators, computerized check-out equipment and a fairly tight security control. The *Times* files were on the second floor and I had to get permission to get up there, and it took some time. The girls who arranged it, however, were charming, and the delay was not altogether unpleasant.

Upstairs I found that the files were on microfilm and I would have to examine them by means of a microfilm reader. I had never had occasion to use such a reader and had to be shown how. I counted back nine years, gave it two more on either side, and went to work out of five boxes of film—one year's issues to the box. That's a lot of newspaper in any town, and the *L. A. Times* is a big one. But I skipped the sports sections, classified ads and editorial sections and stayed with the main news and amusement pages. It took some time to get used to the reader, but once I got it rolling I found I could scan a page in fairly short order. I had to scan closely because the makeup of the *Times* in the edition on file emphasizes dignity rather than sensational display, and the seamy side of life is not especially punched up. Still, I managed to get through the years 1958 and 1959 in about an hour and fifteen minutes. I found no reference to Michele Armande.

I took off my jacket, loosened my tie, tried to find a way to put my feet up but couldn't, and started through 1960. There was nothing to be found on Michele Armande until July, and then suddenly there it was, a short item on a back page.

HOLLYWOOD ACTRESS
DEAD IN ACCIDENT

Michele Armande, actress, died accidentally last night in Inyo County, according to a sheriff's report. The accident occurred during a private party at North Pine Lodge, a hunting and fishing resort. The exact nature of the accident and the identities of other members of the party were not revealed.

Miss Armande appeared in several films between 1956 and 1960 and was most recently seen in a production directed by Ed Fogel. Mr. Fogel's presence at the fatal party was not confirmed. The deceased left no known survivors. She had married actor Peter Rinaldi in 1957, but the marriage is reported to have been annulled in Mexico in 1958. Mr. Rinaldi was not available for comment.

I read the story three or four times, turned off the reader, then turned it on again and browsed through the next half-dozen issues, looking for a follow-up. There was no follow-up in plain sight, but turning back slowly, I found a short item on the obit page. It read:

MICHELE ARMANDE
Services for Hollywood actress Michele Armande, who died in an accident at North Pine Lodge, Inyo County,

were held yesterday at Crestline Mortuary. Services were private and interment took place in Mountain View Memorial Park near North Pine. Attending services were Miss Armande's director, Ed Fogel, a Miss Patricia White and Mr. and Mrs. Sam Fingal, who manage North Pine Lodge.

And that was the extent of that. I wrote down the names Patricia White, Sam Fingal and Mrs. Fingal, put the file back in the box and returned it to the desk. It had taken me two hours to learn not very much about something that had happened long ago and far away.

On my way to the parking lot—a stiff hike from the library—I thought: In view of the news report of eight years before, what was it that actually happened last night in a run-down apartment in Culver City? Explain that to Lieutenant Shapiro.

No way.

One thing I found comforting, though I couldn't say exactly why: my client Peter Rinaldi had not been present at obsequies for Michele Armande.

Peter Rinaldi had left a message with my answering service. The number was not Mary Dane's or Ed Fogel's. It was the number of a cocktail lounge called the Blue Parrot, around the corner from my office. A jukebox was pouring out loud rock and when Rinaldi finally got on the phone I had to ask him to speak up. He spoke up long enough to say he had to see me. I suggested the office and he hesitated, and when I said it sounded as if it would be hard to converse in the place, he agreed to meet me on the corner of Yucca and Vine, a short walk. I couldn't figure out why he was reluctant to come to the office.

Maybe he planned on giving me some more resistance and felt stronger on some ground of his own. He was becoming a strange guy. He made me nervous.

I wasn't any less nervous when, at the corner of Yucca and Vine, I watched him approach with a male companion named Clyde—my Clyde, my freak.

So it must have been Clyde who didn't want to come to the office.

Clyde grinned at me with his slack mouth. Rinaldi seemed to be pretending he didn't know Clyde, had just happened to pick up a stranger in a bar.

We stood there, an uncertain trio, in the shadow of the Capitol Records building, Hollywood's leaning tower of pizza.

"What will it be," I said, "pinochle, hearts, three-handed cribbage?"

Clyde giggled.

"Would you like to give us some privacy?" I said.

He giggled again. I had a very bad thing for him and I didn't feel patient. God knows what was going through his weird mind. He must have thought he had everything wired, there being three of us and his own status equivocal. The corner was well lighted and he wouldn't be likely to launch a confrontation. At the same time, neither would I. The meeting seemed futile, senseless. And yet, Rinaldi had suggested it and somewhere along the way he had picked up Clyde. The somewhere had probably been the Blue Parrot.

"Why did you leave the hospital?" I asked Rinaldi.

"I was feeling all right," he said, "and I really don't have the kind of money it takes—"

"All right," I said. "What did you want to see me about?"

"A related matter," he said. "I don't have the money either to pay a private detective."

I glanced at Clyde, who was grinning slackly. I wished I had a hot cigar to shove between his teeth—backwards.

"Well," I said, "you mean you want me to quit the case?"

"Yes. I think that sums it up," he said.

That summed it up fairly succinctly. The only thing wrong with it was, why did he have to have Clyde in on the kiss-off? I had to conclude that the idea was not exclusively Rinaldi's. Nobody would drag Clyde along for moral support.

"Okay," I said, "whatever you want. I guess that frees me to go to San Diego."

Clyde chuckled. "That's a wise decision," he said.

I glanced around. Nobody seemed to be watching. So I hung one on Clyde, a hard one, on the left side of his jaw, where it would at least knock him down. It was rough on my hand, but it worked. He dropped to the sidewalk. I got my hands under his arms and dragged him behind a low-lying hedge. When I looked around again, nobody appeared to have noticed. Rinaldi was staring at me.

"Come on," I said. "Up to the office."

"Look—" he said.

"Rinaldi, come on!"

He came along then. I walked him as fast as I dared up the street and around the corner to my office building. Clyde didn't show. I didn't like to think about the next time I might see him.

I got Rinaldi into the office and made sure the door was locked. He stood there, not without his old actor's dignity, watching me, waiting.

"Sit down," I said. "Would you like coffee?"

"No, thank you," he said, but he sat down.

"Listen, Rinaldi," I said, "if you tell me again, straight out, without any witnesses, that you want me to lay off this thing about Michele Armande, I will do it. But I'm not going to take it from you in the presence of that freak Clyde. Where did you pick him up?"

For a while I thought he was going to hold out on me again, but finally he slumped a little, his face relaxed and he said, "Actually, he picked me up. I was leaving Ed Fogel's office at the studio and this fellow was waiting for me outside. He said he had a message from Abigail and he had a cab waiting. We rode to the Blue Parrot and he . . . uh . . . suggested I call you."

"Is he pretty suggestive?"

"He's persuasive."

"What was his threat?"

"He said Abigail and her husband were anxious not to embarrass Mary."

"Mary Dane?"

"Yes. They said the publicity about Michele would be an embarrassment and humiliation to her."

"You have any idea how that could be?"

"I didn't have—"

"But Clyde straightened you out?"

"Yes."

"And you were convinced."

"Yes, I was."

"By what he said alone? Did it fit with any knowledge of your own?"

He looked away. "Yes, it did," he said.

"Do you want to tell me about it?"

"No, not really. I don't think it would serve any purpose."

"It would enlighten me."

"Perhaps."

I took a turn around the desk. "I don't know what to think," I said. "I feel I've been imposed on. That vanishing corpse trick is a humdinger. It's going to take time to forget."

"I know absolutely nothing about that."

"Do you have any suspicions?"

"No," he said.

"How did you happen to marry Michele Armande?"

He shrugged. "Impulse," he said, "a middle-aged man's last fling, so to speak. There was an excuse."

"Excuse?"

"She was from France, about to have to return. Marriage to an American citizen would extend her visa indefinitely, and she could apply for citizenship. I guess you could say I took advantage of her quandary."

"But then the marriage was annulled."

His eyes blinked once. "You knew about that?"

"I read that in the *L. A. Times*."

"It's not really accurate. I tried to have it annulled, in Mexico, but it wasn't worth anything in California. I mean, it didn't work. Michele found a lawyer and he blocked it."

"What grounds did you offer for the annulment?"

"I don't remember. It's very loose in Mexico, a matter of bribery."

"Did you really believe Michele died in that accident at North Pine Lodge eight years ago?"

"I believed it, yes. No reason not to."

"You were no longer living with Michele at that time?"

"No. We never did live together in real marriage. A few nights—"

112

"A few nights," I said. "So you didn't have any real grounds for an annulment."

"That's right."

"You told me Michele and Fogel were lovers at one time. Did you marry Michele as a convenience to Fogel?"

He set his mouth and said nothing.

"When did you first learn Michele wasn't dead?"

"A few days ago. Those two—the ones we saw at her apartment—they brought me the news. It was when they told me Michele was alive that I agreed to meet with them."

"Michele was making demands on you?"

"Yes."

"Through those two musclemen?"

"Yes."

"Did you know they worked for Caccelli?"

"I don't know it now."

"I'm telling you now."

"I see," he said.

So there we were again. I see.

"What kind of pressure could Michele put on you?" I asked. "Had you mistreated her?"

"No, never. She demanded money, and she threatened to go to Mary—make a scene—"

"So you were hung up," I said. "You had no money and you couldn't help Michele without going to Mary yourself."

"That's it, yes."

"And the two muscles worked you over some."

"A little."

"What did they want when they picked you up earlier today and dumped you out here?"

"I don't know. All they said to me was, 'Forget about

Michele Armande and tell your friends to forget about her too.' "

"By 'friends,' presumably, they meant me, and possibly Lieutenant Shapiro?"

"I assume—yes."

"Did you have a meeting with Armande yourself, after Caccelli's two guys pushed you around?"

"No," he said. "I was going to visit her last night. She was dead when I got there."

"You never had a chance to speak with her before she died?"

"No," he said firmly.

I circumnavigated the desk again.

"Well, Mr. Rinaldi," I said, "I am at a loss. Since I am at a loss, there isn't much I can do. Therefore, if you still wish it, I will withdraw from this investigation. I'm pretty sure the two musclemen won't bother you again. I can't predict what Clyde may do."

"It's my risk," he said.

"It may not be so great a risk. The scores he has to settle are with me."

"I'm sorry," he said.

"It's all right, part of the job. Do you have money enough to get home?"

"Yes."

"I'll call a taxi and wait with you."

I dialed the Yellow Cab number and ordered the cab, and Rinaldi and I sat around and avoided looking at each other most of the time. It's always uncomfortable to sit around with a client after you've been fired. There are a lot of questions, but you don't want to raise them once you've signed out.

114

"You might give Miss Dane a ring and let her know you're all right," I said.

"Yes," he said.

He picked up the phone and dialed and after a minute I heard him talking to Mary Dane. I didn't try to follow the conversation. Whatever their mutual thing was, it was exclusively theirs. It was evidently tender and a matter of intense loyalty, and there was nothing to do but to admire it. I hoped things would work out all right.

Someone knocked and I asked who it was.

"Taxi," a guy said.

I opened up for him and Rinaldi hung up the phone. We went outside and down the steps and I saw Rinaldi into the cab.

"Good luck," I said.

"Yes—thank you," he said.

They drove away. I walked up and down in front of the office and tried to think myself out of the case, but it was impossible. There were too many loose ends, too many questions.

One of the most troublesome questions was why Caccelli would put enough faith in Clyde to send him on the mission to Rinaldi. It didn't seem to be Clyde's kind of work, and it seemed unlikely that Caccelli would take a chance on him.

So—maybe it hadn't been Caccelli at all, but somebody else.

Who else?

And the most fascinating question was: If Michele Armande had not been laid to rest eight years before in North Pine, California, who had?

I went up to the office and called Shapiro. He wasn't in.

I found someone who would talk to me and conned him into looking up whether Riordan and Dennis had been picked up. He checked it out and said no.

There was a knock at the door.

"Who is it?" I said.

"Abigail Caccelli," she said.

I went over and opened the door and Abigail was outside. She was not alone. With her was Little Joe Caccelli and with the two of them was big Clyde, grinning at me with that mouth. As the door swung open, he stepped forward between Caccelli and Abigail. He had a knife in his right hand, blade out toward my belt. No time left to slam the door on them; Clyde was a step too close. Nothing to do but let them in.

10

I wasn't awfully polite. I was concentrating on a way to disarm Clyde and had little to offer the others.

"Caccelli," I said, "get this monkey off my back. I swear, I'll tie his legs around his neck and dump him off the roof."

"Now, now," Caccelli said, "Clyde doesn't want to hurt anybody."

Every fiber of Clyde's being wanted to hurt somebody —specifically me. He was just out of reach. All he had was a knife, not such a horrendous weapon, except that the way he was holding it, he could put it deep in me simply by letting it fly a short distance, such a short distance. I tried backing off, but he came right along. He was steady on his feet and in his hands, and by my conservative calculations, he was totally unpredictable.

"I had an impression you were going to San Diego," Caccelli said.

"Sure," I said, "when I get some other things wrapped up."

"Like what other things?"

"Confidential other things."

I didn't like talking to him without looking at him. It

was disconcerting and, in a way, demeaning. But I didn't dare take my eyes off Clyde, who kept grinning in that vacuous way.

"I wouldn't worry about it," I said. "If your guy is screwing you, he can't screw you too much in one day."

Clyde shifted the position of his hand slightly and I backed off another step. Clyde came along. I had an idea that if I could get my behind up against the desk, I could use my feet on him. Feet, being encased in leather, are better than hands against a knife.

"Why don't you send Clyde to San Diego?" I said. "I'm sure he could do a better job than I could."

"Very amusing," Caccelli said.

"I wish you'd send him somewhere," I said. "Like to some zoo."

Clyde giggled.

"He must be hungry, too," I said. "He hasn't earned the first twenty dollars yet."

At about the moment my behind came up against the desk, Clyde decided he didn't like that last remark. It was part of my plan. My feet came up when he lunged and it would have worked just fine, but his first pass was a high feint. I missed connecting with him and the next thing I knew I was on my back on the desk with him over me and the knife point digging at my solar plexus. He had my legs pinned against the desk and I couldn't move in any direction nor get enough leverage to sit up. He yanked my shirt up out of my pants and scratched with the knife. I glanced toward Caccelli and found Abigail instead. She was making a suitably horrified face, but her eyes were glazed with anticipation.

She's another one at heart, I thought. A freak. A freak like him. It all fits with Caccelli.

"Call him off, Caccelli," I said.

I could feel blood on my belly now and it felt bad. The sick one was beginning to giggle again.

"Where's your suitcase?" Caccelli said.

"You mean you really want to pack me off to San Diego?"

"Like we agreed," he said.

"The suitcase is in the bedroom closet, through that connecting door."

Clyde started making writing motions with the knife. Caccelli's short-man's footsteps clacked over the floor. They stopped in the other room. I heard the closet door open and the lurch of bedsprings.

"All right, Doll," Caccelli said, "pack him a few things. Shirts, shorts, a toothbrush, razor—"

"Sure," Abigail said happily.

Then I could hear her bustling about in the bedroom. I looked up at Clyde and he was chortling. His hand kept moving.

"You writing a poem or something?" I said.

He giggled.

"You'll book in at the El Cortez," Caccelli was saying, "and get in touch with Sam Goldblatt. I already told him to take you on the rounds. I said I'm breaking in a guy for the territory up north."

Up north, I thought.

"I got it," I said.

A knock at the door. I heard it swing open. Nobody had thought to close it tight after the invasion. A guy said, "What in the name of—?"

"Fogel," Caccelli said, "what do you want here?"

The door closed. Fogel had presence of mind—or automatic responses.

"Are you out of your mind?" he said.

"Just relax," Caccelli said.

It seemed clear that Caccelli didn't know quite what to do about Fogel—and Fogel didn't know how to go about whatever had brought him.

"What brought you here?" Caccelli asked.

"I had a long talk with Peter Rinaldi," Fogel said. "I wanted to talk to Mr.—to Mac about it."

"Go ahead, talk," Caccelli said. "He can talk."

"Not in this position," I said.

"Let him up for God's sake," Fogel said. "This is childish."

Clyde growled in his fat throat.

"Okay, Clyde," Caccelli said, "get off him."

Clyde looked hurt, the way a little kid looks when mommy won't buy him the box of Wheaties with Batman on it. But finally he took his hand off me and drew back with the knife. I sat up, my feet shaking, stuck my shirt back in my pants and kicked my heels against the desk to get the blood started.

"Hello, Mr. Fogel," I said. "What was it about Rinaldi?"

"Well, Peter Rinaldi is one of my oldest friends," he said. "He called me from the hospital—very upset—and I went over there and helped him check out. Then we went to my office and had a talk."

"I see," I said.

Now cut that out, I told myself.

"What did you talk about?" I asked.

"Michele Armande," Fogel said. "I don't know whether you knew it, but Michele was Peter's wife."

"I knew that."

"He thought she had been dead for eight years. So did I. Michele had worked for me a few times—"

"I knew that too," I said, "and that she was reported to be dead eight years ago."

"Well—" Fogel said, "Peter evidently discovered her body in an apartment in Culver City—"

"Right," I said, "just before I turned up."

"Yes. Naturally such a discovery was bad enough. But then, Peter told me, you started hounding him. He said you were conducting a private investigation of the death—which Peter assumed had been suicide—"

"I didn't hound him. I was investigating all right, but not getting any response, especially from Rinaldi. It wasn't a suicide. And then the body disappeared."

Fogel stared at me. "How could a body—? What are you telling me?"

"Peter didn't tell you the body disappeared?"

"Nothing like that. How could it disappear?"

"Well, either she came back to life and wandered off and got lost—or somebody stole her."

"But—why?"

"I don't know why."

He sank into a chair and put his face on one hand. "Oh my God," he said. "No wonder Peter was upset. Such a weird scene—he was badly shaken."

"I've been shaky myself," I said. "What did you think I could help you with?"

"I . . . don't know. It was just that Peter said you wouldn't leave him alone . . . he was worried about the way Mary would take everything . . . Mary Dane."

"I know Miss Dane," I said.

Abigail came out of the bedroom, carrying the suitcase.

Clyde was shifting the knife from hand to hand, looking confused.

"Could I have a couple of Band-Aids?" I said.

"Go get him some Band-Aids," Caccelli said to Abigail.

"Where—what?" she said.

"Look in the goddamned bathroom!" Caccelli yelled.

I jumped a little. It was a surprise to hear such a little guy come out with such a big voice. Clyde jumped too.

"What did you intend to do?" Fogel asked.

"I'm sending him to San Diego," Caccelli said, "where he agreed to do a job for me. And to get him off Rinaldi's back."

Fogel shook his head, got up and wandered unsteadily toward the door. "I think you're out of your mind," he said.

"Go home," Caccelli said, "and take a couple of pills."

Fogel glanced at me briefly, then opened the office door and went out. I sat with my legs dangling and looked at Abigail. She looked at something else.

"Caccelli—" I said, "who stole the corpse from Culver City?"

"How in hell would I know?" he said.

"It couldn't have been Clyde," I said. "He would have goofed it up some way."

Clyde started for me with the knife out.

"No!" Caccelli barked at him.

Clyde stopped, but worked me over with his eyes and his dirty mouth.

Abigail handed me a couple of Band-Aids. I opened my shirt and there were two scratches, neither serious. The bleeding had stopped, but it was messy down there. Still, it seemed a waste of time to take a bath. Maybe in

San Diego, at the El Cortez Hotel—if I should get as far as San Diego.

In a burst of irrelevance I found myself wondering why Rinaldi hadn't brought Fogel with him to the Blue Parrot. Or maybe he had been with Fogel and Clyde had somehow separated them. But it was hard to see Clyde being that clever. I had a wistful hope that Fogel was somewhere calling somebody to come to my assistance, but it wasn't much of a hope. He and Caccelli had business dealings; Fogel wouldn't put the cops on him.

"Okay, let's go," Caccelli said.

His tone was definite and unappealable. I had a gun in the bottom drawer of my desk, but it might as well have been in the next county. Clyde had the knife and he knew how to use it and he had piled up plenty of grievances. When he flashed it at me, I started walking. Caccelli picked up the suitcase, took Abigail's arm and I heard them coming along behind us.

"The back steps," Caccelli barked.

I started down that way. Clyde was on top of everything now. There were no escape routes on that sealed-in stairway. There was the exit door at the street level and I thought about that, but not with great hope. If it had been Clyde alone I might figure on getting through it fast enough to slam it on him. But Caccelli would have thought of it too.

He had. I hit the square landing at the bottom of the stairs and Caccelli said, "Hold it."

I stopped and Clyde came up against me hard. I could feel the point of the knife digging at my kidney region. It didn't draw blood. I didn't want it to draw blood. I stood still and minded my manners.

Caccelli walked around us, pushed the door open and stood outside, holding it. The knife jabbed at me.

"Your car," Caccelli said, "back seat."

He opened the left rear door and I got in. One wild moment of hope. I might get all the way across and out the other door. But the hope died. Clyde was in beside me before I could reach the door handle, and the knife poked at my left ribs. The guy was wild. At the slightest provocation—maybe no provocation at all—he would run it into me as deep as it would go. And take his chances on the rap. It was at that moment, I think, I understood the crucial thing about him. Not only was he wild, a freak —he was a suicidal freak.

Caccelli was opening the front door and throwing the suitcase onto the right side of the seat.

"Get in, Doll," he said.

Abigail got under the wheel. Lovely Abigail with the silver hair and the ecstatic expression. She was a freak too, and quite possibly suicidal. The pair of them made Riordan and Dennis look like good guys in comparison.

"Give her the key," Caccelli said to me.

I hesitated. The knife jabbed at my flank. I reached into my pocket and found the key. Abigail's hand was lifted and open on the back of the seat. I laid the key in it and settled back, trying to edge away from Clyde. It was like trying to edge away from a mudslide.

"Drive carefully," Caccelli said. "Call me from the El Cortez."

"Sure, honey," Abigail said.

Caccelli closed the door. Abigail found the starter and the engine came to life. She had to experiment some to find reverse gear, but she found it and shifted roughly and backed into the alley. Then we straightened out and she had the gears all right and we headed into the street and turned left to make the two blocks to the Hollywood Freeway on-ramp. We made it without a stop and got up there, and the lights of Hollywood began to fade behind us.

11

You SEE things in the movies, or read about them in other books—the unwilling victim of abduction heroically freeing himself by:

1—laying a snow job on the fair damsel who's helping to execute the plan, so she will betray her partner and free the prisoner; or

2—kneeing the car door open and hurling himself out (at eighty m.p.h.), rolling over and over down an embankment—and living through it; or

3—subtly inducing sloth in the man with the weapon, overpowering him, seizing the weapon and using it to force the fair damsel to stop the car; or

4—sending Morse code signals with a cigaret lighter and alerting a passing highway patrolman; or

5—painfully insinuating his hand backward between the seat and the back of the seat (while his arm grows longer and longer), finding the proper wiring and ripping it out, forcing the car to a stop; or

But why go on? What you really do is to sit there in your own sweat and wait, and hope—and maybe pray—for a break. A break could come with a blowout (a doubtful break at eighty m.p.h.), with a traffic violation on the part of the fair driver, causing the highway patrol to pull her over, or running out of gas, or running into a road block set up by astute officers for someone else. If no break occurs, you go on sitting there, waiting for the other end of the trip. I couldn't see how they were going to handle it, marching me into the El Cortez at knifepoint and forcing me to register. But Caccelli had probably figured that out too.

Caccelli also could have figured that Clyde might crack up along the way and put me to sleep permanently, and that would accomplish Caccelli's purpose as well as or better than the phony assignment to check out Sam Goldblatt, who was probably now sitting in some cool, comfortable saloon, listening to the jukebox and counting his day's take.

Abigail was a good driver, speedy but not reckless. She probably wasn't doing eighty m.p.h. That would sooner or later bring on a police halt. But she tooled it along at a steady sixty-eight or seventy, and she could no doubt get away with that all right. She didn't cut in and out or change lanes without warning or do any of the other bad things people do on freeways. She didn't even smoke cigarets. Her high-curled silver hair gleamed in the night lights, and she spoke not a word.

Clyde spoke a few words. They were unintelligible at first, low, grumbling sounds and I didn't try to make them out. But then he got warmed up and began to come in clearer.

"I could kill you easy," he said.

"I know," I said.

"I'd dig that, man. It would be groovy . . . open you up and let the blood run out . . . "

"Sure. Groovy."

Silence for a while. The car grooved steadily south on the freeway, past Triggs Street, merged into the Santa Ana Freeway, headed for Orange County.

"But I'm supposed to see you make it to San Diego," he said. "So you won't make it tough, huh?"

"Of course not," I said.

He dug at me in a cursory way with the knife point.

"Very sharp knife," he said, "long . . . six-inch blade, razor sharp. Nice for cutting."

"I've admired it," I said.

"Don't get smart-ass," he said.

"Excuse me."

"We just ride along and not make any trouble," he said, "because . . . you start doing a thing, see, I'll have to cut on you."

"I won't start doing a thing, honest," I said.

He giggled. "I know, man, because, see, I would cut a little bit at a time, piece here, piece there, and you wouldn't want to die that way, so you wouldn't start doing a thing."

"I don't want to die in any way at all," I said.

He chortled. "You don't dig that, huh?"

"No siree, old buddy," I said.

The knife dug hard at me. It almost drew blood. Clyde didn't want any more of the jokes.

Under ordinary circumstances, that kind of blood-talk, you can shrug it off, pay no attention. But the circumstances weren't ordinary and he was bugging me. I was more afraid of getting buggy than I was of him and his knife. When bugged bad enough, a man will do foolish things, such as trying to create a break that isn't due to come along. I got a grip on myself, tried to relax in the

128

seat but couldn't and settled for staring out the window and nodding my head whenever Clyde opened his yap, which was often.

We were past Paramount, heading for the intricate interchange at Santa Ana–Orange. The traffic had thinned and was continuing to thin, mile by mile. That made more remote the chance for a break. The car had plenty of gas —I had filled it that morning. The only things that could force us to stop were: 1—flat tire, 2—cops, or 3— engine failure. Engine failure was unlikely. I had bought a complete tune-up job three days before. And the way Abigail was driving, a police stop was almost unthinkable.

Clyde was muttering something and I felt a surge of heat, then forced myself to listen.

"You were a pretty tough guy the first time," he said, "but you ain't so tough now, huh?"

"I'm not tough at all," I said. "I think I'll just go to sleep."

"You ain't that cool either," he said. "You can't go to sleep because I might kill you while you were sleeping."

"That's possible," I said.

"No, I wouldn't do that," he giggled. "I'd wake you up first. That way it's more groovy."

I didn't like the way he used the present tense. I wondered how many times he had grooved in that way.

We had the highway virtually to ourselves now, coming into the stretch between Santa Ana and San Clemente, where the route is a precise straight line for about twelve miles and then you hit the hills of San Juan Capistrano. I sat still in the seat, wishing I could sleep, knowing I couldn't, riding it out, listening to Clyde's heavy breathing close to my ear. His breath was bad.

129

I wonder if I could take him, right here in the back seat? I asked myself about fifty times.

Bad chances, I told myself. There's not room enough—even a slight miscalculation and he could cut me very deep, if not fatally, and if he got his blood up, he'd probably finish me off in the excitement, because it would be groovy.

I tried reasoning with myself.

You resigned the case, at Rinaldi's insistence, I thought. You don't have any urgent appointments. Ride it out to San Diego—another hour or so—and then get home eventually and look for something to do.

But there was a sweat, a thing pushing hard at my head, a question, a whole series of questions, and they had an urgency.

Where was the body of Michele Armande?

Why had Rinaldi been so insistent, even when out from under Clyde's pressure, even when he was alone?

Why had Caccelli, caught in a violent act, let Ed Fogel wander away, possibly to call the cops?

Maybe Caccelli, for some reason, was invulnerable to the cops and Shapiro would never admit it. Unlikely.

Although, come to think of it, all Lou had said when I suggested words with Caccelli was, "In due time, in due time."

If he was covered on every count, why was Caccelli so determined to get me out of town, out of action?

That body hanging from the bedpost in the Culver City apartment, that woman—was it really Michele Armande? The only thing I had to go on was Rinaldi's word, and Rinaldi's position was, to put it mildly, ambiguous.

There had been the conversation in the beer tavern, the proprietor and the patrons who made jokes about her as a movie queen. But that had been based on what Michele, or whoever she was, had told them. People make things up.

There was something else, too, more urgent than these questions. There was Mary Dane. Rinaldi had seemed to be solicitous of Mary Dane's feelings. But if Rinaldi was playing a wild, dangerous game, what about Mary Dane if his game went wrong? I had an arrangement with Mary Dane. She hadn't told me to quit. I owed her what I could manage. And besides, I liked Mary Dane. What could I do for Mary Dane in San Diego? Damn little.

So there was a sweat.

We slowed suddenly and both Clyde and I lurched in the seat. The knife was right there, though. I could feel it dig at my ribs. If I had turned on him at that moment, he would have pushed it through my heart.

The cause of the slowing was a momentary traffic tie-up near the Laguna Beach turn-off. Unhappily it was only a matter of congestion. No accident. No stop. So that didn't help me. After about two and a half minutes we were in the clear again, heading into the mountains-palisades area of Capistrano. Here the highway wound and climbed between the brown hills on the inland side and the palisades on the ocean side. They rose from twenty-five to sixty or seventy feet from the water, where the surf broke white against the rocks.

For the first time since she had said goodbye to Caccelli, more than an hour before, Abigail said something.

"Hey, Clyde—?" she said.

"Yeah," he said.

"You want to drive all the way to San Diego?"

"Uh . . . no," he said, and giggled.

"Neither do I."

A short time passed, such a short time.

"We could let him walk home," Abigail said.

Clyde chuckled. "Yeah," he said, "if he can still walk."

"Now Clyde—" she said.

Clyde giggled himself almost into hysterics. I'd have been closer to hysterics myself if I hadn't been so curious to know how they planned to dump me.

The car slowed again and now it boded less than good. An occasional car passed us in one direction or the other, but for the most part we were alone on the highway. The hills were high and dark on the left and the moonless sky over the water was opaque and heavy-looking.

Again we slowed, the brakes grabbed, throwing me forward. But they threw Clyde forward at the same time and the knife slid sharp along my lower left ribs.

If only they weren't such crazies, I thought.

An idle thought if ever I had one.

Abigail stopped altogether, we lurched forward, then backward as she turned right, climbing a narrow utility road toward the palisades. We were about fifty feet from the outside edge, but the road twisted sharply, and after two turns we were out of sight of the highway. There was a small fenced enclosure which I took for a power station. Aside from that, there was nothing but gravel and the rest of the brief ascent to the edge of the cliff. Below that would be the ocean—far below that.

Abigail stopped the car about ten feet from the fenced, concrete blockhouse. She cut the lights and opened the car door on her side, saying, "Let's not fool around over it."

Clyde chuckled. The knife point nudged me. "Open the door," he said.

Abigail had anticipated him, either from smarts in the

132

head or stupidity. If one, there would be lots of trouble for me; if the other—it could be the break. She opened the door wide and held it open. She was smart enough to stand behind it, well out of my reach. I had only one way to go and I would have to go fast, very fast.

I swung my right leg out the door, got my heel on the sill, pulled against the jamb with my right hand and dived out of the car. For the first time, the knife point was clear of me. I hit the ground with my left foot, started to sprint, stumbled over a loose rock and came up against the steel fence with my right shoulder, twisting as I hit. Clyde was on top of me, his left arm up and bent against my neck to push me hard into the fence. I felt the knife go into my left arm, inside. My knee came up into his lower belly and I hit him as hard as I ever hit anyone in my life, just under the ribs, driving upward. It pushed him off. He yanked the knife out of me roughly and came back. I kicked him in the stomach and swung on him from the left and he went down on his hands and knees. He still had hold of the knife.

I jumped to get my foot on his hand, but he got it out of the way in time and lunged up at me. I hit him in the face a few times and he tried to slash me, but I was moving pretty well. I kicked him in the jaw and he let go of the knife. I couldn't see where it went. But the hell with it, I thought. He was not so glass-jawed as my earlier experience had indicated. My kick barely bothered him, except for the loss of the knife, which equalized us more or less. I had lost more blood than he—so far.

He came on more carefully this time, hunched in the shoulders. All the pent-up frustration and pain and rage I had cost him in the last few hours came out in bellowing. He roared as he swung a wide right fist at me. I ducked that one and hammered his chest and neck, and he got his left arm around my neck. We went down and rolled in the gravel and he was kneeing me very bad and low down. I pushed him over and tried to get his nose with the heel of my hand, but he moved his head clear and threw me off. When I managed to scramble up, he was waiting for me.

I moved a couple of steps, turning, trying to get my breath and to find out where Abigail was. She was off to my right, picking up the knife.

"Gimme," Clyde said.

She started toward him with the knife, holding it by the blade, offering it to him. She was closer to him than I was, but I had more to lose. I went for Clyde, whose attention was divided, and hit him half a dozen short left and right hooks with the power I had left. He went down all right, but when I turned, Abigail had got hold of the knife handle and was lifting it. I would have laughed if I'd had the breath for it.

"Don't be silly," I gasped.

She didn't know what she was doing. She stared at me, holding the knife up as if to hit me with it somehow. I reached for her wrist, caught and squeezed it hard and, after a moment, the knife dropped. I let go of her, stooped and picked up the knife and looked at Clyde, who was getting up, but slowly. I was high with exertion and relief, and this time I did laugh, right in his face.

"Come on," I said, "let's be groovy."

He came, bellowing. He had some distance to pick up momentum and I stepped aside and let him bang into the steel fence. He clung to it like a beleaguered gorilla, sucking in breath, and I waited. Abigail picked up a rock and threw it at me. It hit me in the thigh and I laughed. Clyde turned to look at me. I tossed the knife over the edge of the cliff and started for him.

"Come on," I said, "bare hands. That's really the grooviest of all."

He just hung there, clinging to the fence. I hit him hard, once, in the soft of his abdomen, and he hung on, holding himself up. I couldn't make myself hit him again. A time comes when it's all over. I had freaked out for a while, along with him, but I was not a freak for real. I could feel the cut in my arm now and the gravel under my shoes, and the wind was blowing cold off the ocean and everything was real.

"Abigail, get in the car," I said. "Put the suitcase in the back and get in the front seat."

"No," she said.

"All right, then stay and walk home with Clyde."

I went to the car and neither of them moved. Clyde hung on to the fence. Abigail watched me. I got under the wheel, got the thing started, backed and started to turn. She yelled at me and when I looked she was coming on the run. I threw the bag into the back seat, opened the door for her and she got in.

"Listen," she said, "you can't just go away and leave him—"

"See if I can't," I said.

I found the road and headed toward the highway. Looking back for a moment, I saw Clyde standing by the fence, slumped forward, holding his chest with both arms.

"You're not human," she said. "You're just an animal."

"Yup," I said. "You reason your way and I will reason mine."

I got onto the highway and headed for Los Angeles.

"What are you going to do with me?" she said

"Well, there are a number of things I could do. I could drop you off at the all-night gas station at El Toro and you could call a taxi. Or I could let you out along here and let you hitchhike home. Or we could find a phone booth and call Little Joe Caccelli and you could ask him what we ought to do."

She didn't say anything. Maybe she didn't take me seriously.

"But you are Mary Dane's daughter," I said, "and I have a fondness for Mary Dane. So I'm going to take you home to her, and I guess you could call Little Joe from there and have him pick you up."

"Don't call him Little Joe!" she yelled.

"Okay," I said. "What do you call him? Snookums?"

"He was only trying to help me, help my career!"

"Oh," I said. "I misinterpreted everything."

"She's not my real mother anyway," she said.

"That seems clear," I said.

"Oh, shut up," she said.

"Now you're talking," I said. "Now, baby, you are grooving."

And neither of us said anything more to each other the rest of that dreary ride.

12

I DROVE up to Mary Dane's gate, got out, opened the gate, got back in the car and drove inside. Then I got out again and closed the gate and then I opened the door for Abigail. After a while, she got out.

"Listen," she said, "please—don't make me go in there. You go and call Joe and tell him to come and get me. I'll wait out here."

"You do me grave injustice," I said. "Either you impugn my sense of chivalry or you question my good sense. For two reasons I won't do as you ask. Number one, I would never leave a young lady standing around in the cold waiting for a ride, and number two, I'm convinced that if I should leave you out here while I go in and make the call, you would get in my car and run over me at the first opportunity."

Her lip trembled. Her hand fluttered toward me. I decided she had the makings of an actress after all.

"Please—" she said, "she's been so good to me. If you tell her about tonight—that wild ride and all—it will kill her."

"You can't stop hurting me, can you?" I said. "It

wouldn't kill her—you just don't know her. But I won't
tell her a thing except that you want to call Joe. And
when you tell Joe, you're welcome to say anything you
like as far as I am concerned. Now let's cut out the chatter
and get inside, because it's cold out here and I've got lots
to do. That's a good girl. Come along."

I tried to take her arm, in a friendly way, but she
snatched it away and marched off ahead of me. I started
to ring the bell but she shook her head, reached up into a
slot under the door light and brought down a key. She
opened the door, we went in and she ducked into an
alcove near the reception entry to our left. There would
be, I assumed, a telephone in there and she could avoid
seeing Mary Dane if she was lucky.

I saw a light at the stairs across the checkerboard floor
of the hall and started over there.

"Miss Dane?" I called.

Her voice came distantly from her room at the bottom
of the stairs.

"Yes?"

"It's me, Mac," I said.

"Please come down," she said.

At the top of the stairs I looked back across the big, dim
room. Abigail was standing near the alcove, watching
me. I waved at her and started down. Three steps and I
reached out for support. The night was catching up with
me. I was lightheaded and wondered whether I had lost
more blood than I could afford. There was quite a sticky
mess under my arm where Clyde had got to me. It seemed
not to be flowing anymore though.

I went down the rest of the way and Miss Dane was
sitting in her reading chair, looking at a magazine. I

couldn't tell what magazine it was. My vision was on the blurred side.

"My goodness," she said.

"I apologize for my appearance," I said. "It has been a hectic evening. But I wanted to see you, and especially to see Peter, if he's here."

"Oh yes, I'm sure he's here. He came home several hours ago. He was very tired and went straight to bed."

"I hate to wake him, but it's urgent."

"Of course. I'll show you the way."

I couldn't help admiring the spring in her step when she got up from the chair, no hesitation, no groaning. I couldn't remember whether I ought to go up ahead of her or not—some vague sense of childhood training about following females up the stairs. But it was no problem for her. She just went over there and started up and then I went up and I wasn't thinking about anything except what I wanted to ask Peter Rinaldi, and hoping we could get there before gangrene set in in my arm.

On the main hall level, Abigail was no longer in sight. I had a hunch she was hiding in the alcove. Halfway across the floor, Mary Dane stopped and I almost ran her down.

"It's a horribly large house, isn't it?" she said.

"It's a very nice house."

"I know, but it's—so big!"

"Well, nobody can have everything."

"Yes, isn't that true."

I was surprised to be led then in an upward direction. From the street, the house seemed to descend the canyon wall. But Mary Dane led me to a spiral staircase lifting from a cramped, closet-like landing.

They built houses funny in those days, I thought.

We spiraled upward, me hanging tight to the iron railing. It was the kind of staircase you find backstage, in a corner, a way up to the catwalk. At the top was a narrow iron door, with a knocker. Mary lifted it and I heard a faint clang inside.

"Yes . . . ?" Peter Rinaldi said.

"Peter . . . " Mary said, "I'm sorry to disturb you, but it's Mac. He wants to talk to you."

A fairly long silence. Then, "Of course, just a moment."

It wasn't long to wait. I heard a lock click and the door opened and Rinaldi was standing there in a long, velvet-collared dressing gown, in sandals, blinking a little in the dim light.

"I'll leave you two," Mary Dane said, "good night."

"Good night," I said, "and thanks."

The room was Spartan bare. There was a chair next to a dresser, a window which I judged opened on the ocean side of the house, but the curtains were drawn tight and I couldn't be sure of my bearings after the spiraling climb. There were some pictures on the wall, old-style publicity photos, and nothing much else aside from the few personal items a man living alone needs to get through the day.

I sat in the chair and Rinaldi leaned against the dresser and listened.

"It's like this," I said. "Joe Caccelli and a freak he hires —well, you know who that is—took me for a sort of a ride tonight. I got to wondering about things, and in the course of events I got out from under that trip and came back here. I know you want me off the case, for reasons of your own. But at the same time you didn't actually hire me.

140

Somebody else did, and so there's still a thing working, if you know what I mean."

Rinaldi nodded.

"I understand," he said. "What did you want to ask me?"

"For one thing, didn't it ever occur to you—over the past few hours, that is—that you were in line to be a fall guy, that you might be in a frame?"

"No," he said. "It didn't occur to me. I can't imagine such a thing."

"You would make a good one," I said. "I thought at first that you probably killed Michele. There were logical reasons."

"I suppose that might be," he said.

"All right, let that pass. Another thing—did you ever spend any time at a place called North Pine Lodge?"

He was leaning there with his hands in the pockets of his dressing gown and he smiled a little, then looked at one of the walls for a while and finally he said, "Not very much. I've been there a few times, but not recently. It was a fashionable place for a while—a small group of us used to go up there. But that was some time ago."

"You weren't there when Michele Armande, or someone, suffered a fatal accident?"

"No," he said. He was quite firm.

"Nor three days later when funeral services were held in the vicinity?"

"No. I wasn't even informed that she had died until after it was all over."

"Okay. Did you ever know a girl named Patricia White —for instance, up at North Pine Lodge? Did you ever hear of such a girl?"

"No," he said, "I never did."

"Never met such a person?"

"No, never."

"All right. One more thing, at the risk of sounding repetitious—about the scene we shared last night, at the apartment in Culver City. Was that girl—the woman hanging from the bedpost—Michele Armande?"

He looked straight at me. "Yes," he said. "It was Michele."

"The woman you once married."

"Yes."

"You couldn't be mistaken about it?"

"No."

"It was Michele we saw hanging there last night?"

"Yes."

"For real."

"For real."

I got up. "All right," I said, "thanks for leveling with me."

He shrugged.

"Go back to bed," I said, "get a good night's sleep."

"Thank you."

I got to the door.

"Mac—" he said.

"Yeah?"

"You find out, will you? Go ahead and find out what happened."

I didn't want to turn around and look at him. The spell was working well enough. Sufficient unto the day—

"I'll try," I said.

I started down the spiral staircase, hanging on very tight all the way. Downstairs there was no sign of Mary

Dane. The light was out below the stairs. No sign of Abigail.

I let myself out that door and my car was where I had left it. I had to open the gate, back out, and then close the gate behind me. But that was all right. Everything was all right now.

That is to say—in a tentative way.

I wonder, I thought, as I drove away down the canyon, what broke Peter Rinaldi free? What loosened him?

Not that there had to be any great event. It was probably a state of mind, an evolution of the senses.

That was probably what it was, I kept thinking, sure in my soul that I had discovered a fine new concept, an evolution of the senses.

I stopped at the UCLA Emergency Hospital and spent about half an hour getting my arm treated, along with a shot against infection and another shot of pep medicine. I had to fight for it, but I got it. Back in the car I pondered the wisdom of going home and changing out of my beat-up clothes, but a look at my watch and a glance at the suitcase Abigail had so kindly packed for me turned me off that thinking. I got onto the San Diego Freeway, heading for Culver City.

At the Back Room there was a pool game in progress and business was lively. I saw that they had a waitress who bore no resemblance to Michele Armande, which was a sort of comfort. The proprietor, Harry, busy drawing beer, looked at me five times without recognition. Then he got a break and looked at me again and apparently remembered my face.

"I see you found a waitress," I said.

He nodded again.

"Michele never showed up?"

"Never showed," he said.

He drew me a beer and I drank some of it.

"Was she really Michele Armande the actresss?"

"I don't know," he said. "That's what she said."

"That's the only information you ever had about that, just what she said?"

"That's all," he said.

"Do you have a phone?"

He pointed toward the back of the room, beyond the pool table. I went back there, fed a dime to the slot and dialed Lieutenant Shapiro's number at headquarters. The Lieutenant was off duty.

"Could you give me his home telephone?" I asked.

"No."

"Even if you check me out? He must have a list you can check. I might be on it."

"Well . . . it's late. Could you talk to somebody else?"

"Yes, but nobody else would know what I was talking about."

"What's your name?"

I told him.

"Just a minute," he said.

Pretty soon he came on again and gave me Shapiro's number. I hung up and dialed it. A woman answered.

"Mrs. Shapiro?" I said.

A sharp pause. "Whom did you want?" she asked.

A smart policeman's wife. "Lieutenant Shapiro," I said. "I'm Mac, a private detective. I got the number from headquarters."

"Well—he's asleep," she said.

"I wouldn't wake him, but it's important."

"All right, just a minute."

I waited a while and then another phone lifted and Shapiro spoke sleepily.

"Mac," I said, "sorry to wake you."

"Okay, go ahead."

"Did you ever pick up those two guys Riordan and Dennis?"

"No," he said, "nor hide nor hair."

"And you didn't find their truck?"

"No. Is that all you wanted?"

"Not quite. I wanted to let you know I'm prepared to sign a complaint against Caccelli."

"For what?"

"Kidnapping."

A pause. "You wouldn't take advantage of a tired cop when he's flat on his back, would you?"

"No. But don't get up. I don't have to do it tonight. But so you know I'm ready. One more thing."

"Yes?"

"Could you start running an R and I on a woman named Patricia White, who evidently lived, not too long ago, in that same apartment in Culver City—the one—"

"I know the one. Patricia White?"

"That's it."

"If you say so, if it's for real."

"It's for real."

"Okay. Where are you?"

"The Back Room, a beer tavern, remember?"

"You'll be there awhile?"

"Nope. I'm going hunting."

"Mac—"

"Up north. I'll check in later."

"Listen—"

"Get your sleep, Lieutenant," I said. "I'll stay in touch."

"I'm afraid you will," he said.

I hung up, left the tavern and drove to the apartment on Redgrave Avenue. It was dark. I tried the front door, but it was locked. I drove half around the block, found the alley behind the building and drove up to the back door. It opened directly onto the alley and it, too, was locked.

I got back in the car, got out my California road map and studied it for a while, left it open on the front seat and made a note of the time, 1:08 in the morning, and of the reading on the mileage indicator, 22,387.

I drove away from there onto the freeway, heading north toward Bakersfield, and after a few minutes I was settled into the long night ride. My arm ached badly and I rested it most of the time, moving it periodically to keep the circulation up.

13

It is cold in the hunting season in the foothills of the
Sierra Nevada. It is especially cold at 7:45 in the morning,
after five and a half hours of steady driving, with the last
coffee break two hours gone. I was stiff in every muscle
and especially in the left arm. I tried swinging it around
as I got out in the little county seat town and went into a
cafe called the Mountain View Inn. I didn't try for long;
it hurt too much.

From inside, seated at a front window, I had a view of
Mount Whitney, fourteen and a half thousand feet high
and top-heavy with snow. A waitress brought me coffee
and a menu and I ordered enough breakfast for three
guys. I wasn't sure I could eat all of it, but I didn't want
to run out.

While I waited for the fruit juice, I composed a tele-
gram to the biggest and best skip tracer firm in the country, headquarters Chicago. It was a long shot but not a
reckless one. I addressed the wire to a man I had done
business with, Roy Rowley, and signed it with my full
name. The message read:

ALL YOU CAN FIND ON PATRICA WHITE, FEMALE. LAST SEEN ON RECORD IN INYO COUNTY CALIFORNIA EIGHT YEARS AGO. THAT'S ALL I'VE GOT. REPLY COLLECT SOON AS POSSIBLE TO WESTERN UNION.

It seemed a skimpy lead to give someone, but you would be surprised how much a good skip tracer can find from even less information.

The fruit juice burned my throat and I swallowed coffee to chase it. The oatmeal was soothing and the bacon and eggs were strengthening. When I finished and had downed a couple of pep pills, I felt almost good. The arm hurt, but it was bound to hurt for a while.

"Where could I buy a hunting license?" I asked the waitress.

"Some of the stores sell them," she said, "but they're probably sold out now. You're late, aren't you?"

"Yeah, but maybe I'll catch a few late birds."

"Good luck," she said.

Outside the air was still brisk, but warmer than when I had arrived, though it was clear my suit jacket would be insufficient protection. On the way to Western Union I passed a sporting goods store with a sign that read OPEN. I filed the wire to Roy Rowley and walked back to the store, where I bought a hunting jacket and cap and an inexpensive .30-caliber rifle. I must have looked like the kind of dude you see in the movies. The clerk looked quizzically at my torn and tattered suit jacket, but when I came up with cash he desisted.

"You sell licenses?" I asked.

"Yes," he said, "but we're out of them. You can get one at the courthouse, be open in about an hour."

I walked out into the crisp sunshine in my brand new jacket and cap with my brand new cheap gun under my arm.

It would be fun, I thought, to be really going hunting and nothing else to think about.

I put the gun in the car, went into a drugstore, found a phone booth and looked up North Pine Lodge. The number was a local call. I asked the clerk at the tobacco counter how to get there.

"You go three miles south," she said, "turn right on South Ridge Road, and then about five miles to the junction. I hope you have a reservation. Everything's pretty well filled up."

"I'll take my chances," I said.

She looked doubtful.

"Do you have any suggestions," I asked, "in case the lodge is filled up?"

She spread her hands. "I don't know of a thing anywhere in town," she said. "You might call Mike Van Ness. He has a place not far from North Pine. It's pretty rustic, but I think he puts people up from time to time."

"Mike Van Ness," I said, "thanks."

I wandered around the streets for a while, looked at the big mountain, surreptitiously rubbed my hunting cap against a couple of dusty walls to give it some age, and finally the courthouse opened.

It was a fine, old-fashioned courthouse of brown brick, set back from the street and shaded by tall trees. The hunting licenses were for sale at a window just inside the main entrance, and there was no waiting line. The guy who sold it to me was a friendly, wizened codger in a green eyeshade.

"Kinda tardy, ain't you?" he said. "Usually get these things a month in advance."

"It was a last-minute decision," I said. "I'll take what I can find."

"Yeah, well, good luck."

"Say," I said, "which way to the county clerk's office? Old friend of mine I'd like to look up."

"Right down this hall and downstairs—it's in the basement," he said.

I walked away at a leisurely pace. He must have seen me as the most lackadaisical hunter in the history of the county. As a matter of fact, the more I thought about it, the less I looked forward to roaming through unfamiliar woodlands with a thousand or more city-bred sharpshooters taking aim in all directions.

At the clerk's office I asked to see the death certificates for the year 1960.

"We keep them by quarters," the clerk said.

All I could remember was that the newspaper story had been dated in summer.

"Third quarter," I said.

He went away and returned with a thick spring binder about six by ten inches. It was labeled: *DEATH CERTS. 1960–63.*

"Can't let it away from here," he said.

"That's all right."

I leafed through it rapidly while he watched me. The certificates were in chronological order, and I couldn't remember the dateline of the news story. The notes I had on it were in my suit jacket, which I had left in the car with my gun.

I did find Michele Armande at length, about halfway through the sheaf. The clerk kept watching me and I flipped past the Michele Armande entry for three or four pages and then the telephone rang. The clerk turned away to answer it and I went back to the death certificate of Michele Armande.

She was named, her age was given as thirty-one, the cause of death was given as accidental brain damage. The place was North Pine Lodge. The certificate was signed by the coroner, a Conrad Jackson, and cosigned by Jack Keyhoe, Deputy Sheriff. A longhand note had been scrawled diagonally across the upper right corner of the sheet. I made it out as: 1st officer on scene, Mike Van Ness."

I closed the book and pushed it back to the clerk.

"Couple of old friends I'd like to look up," I said, "Jack Keyhoe for one, used to be with the police—"

"Jack's dead," the clerk said, "died in a car accident a couple of years ago."

"I'm sorry to hear it. There's another guy—Mike Van Ness."

The clerk's eyes grew a thin veil. "Yeah, he's got a place down south a ways. He's not on the force anymore."

"Can you tell me how to get to his place?"

"Well—you go south here to the Y—gas station at North Pine, then you turn off west a ways, couple of miles, and it's up in the woods there. He's got a mailbox out on the road."

"Okay, thanks very much."

I went to my car, drove around the block, paused at the Western Union office and decided Roy Rowley hadn't had enough time even to make a phone call, and went on to the highway leading south. I came to the gas station at the crossroads called North Pine, hesitated and turned west on South Ridge Road. Four and a half miles down the road was the junction and a leaning wooden sign with an arrow pointed down an angling blacktop road to: NORTH PINE LODGE—3 mi.

The road was in good condition and showed signs of recent travel, mostly paper litter that hadn't had time to get yellow yet; and fresh tracks of a heavy vehicle, probably a tractor. There were trees on both sides and no place to turn off. I saw no sign of small game and decided the animals were wise and had left the area.

I rounded a slow curve, the trees scattered and I drove into a large clearing, occupied by a rambling, ranch-style cabin, some outbuildings, and about ten cars and station wagons in various stages of travel dustiness. A wooden sign beside the entrance drive read: NORTH PINE LODGE—PROP. SAM FINGAL.

The main entrance to the lodge was in the center portion of the L-shaped building, where a hand-lettered sign in a window read: OFFICE. I pulled up, left the car and went in there. A woman was pushing a dust-mop over the floor of the cramped office. Beyond, the room opened into a lodge sitting room with a big fireplace and in one corner a small bar. There were leather chairs and divans here and there.

The woman was tired and fiftyish, with stringy hair. She was stringy all over, in fact, like a doll made of pipe cleaners.

"Is Mr. Fingal in?" I asked.

"Yes," she said, barely glancing at me, "but if you're looking for a room, we're all filled up."

"Oh—I was afraid you might be."

She made no suggestions and I hung around.

"Do you suppose I could buy a drink before I travel on?" I asked.

"I guess so—the bar don't really open till eleven." Her voice lifted. "Sam!" she called. "Sam—man wants a drink."

A male voice answered from some distance, but I couldn't make out the words. There were footsteps and a door opened on the far side of the lodge room. The guy who came in was tall and thick, badly musclebound and with a good-sized potbelly. He wore a plaid lumberjacket and a hunting cap and carried a bucket in one hand and a couple of bottles in the other. He glanced my way, crossed the room to the bar and set down the bottles. I heard him dumping ice into a can behind the bar. I walked over there, taking my time. On the wall opposite the fireplace were glossy photos, most of them with inscriptions. I veered that way and saw that they were Hollywood photos. I wasn't close enough to make out faces or read the inscriptions.

Sam Fingal's face was blotched by some skin defect, and there were blotches on the backs of his hands. Aside from that he was a well-built, though overmuscled, guy with short clipped gray hair showing under the turned-up flaps of his cap.

"Sam Fingal?" I said.

"That's me," he said, "what did you want?"

"I wanted a room," I said, "but I'm told you're filled up."

"Oh hell yes, booked solid a month ago. Said you wanted a drink?"

"If I may—bourbon and water."

"Sure."

He put ice in a glass, poured bourbon into it liberally and filled it with water from a tap. I put a dollar on the bar and he put it away without giving me change.

"No way at all you could accommodate me?" I said.

"Unless you want to sleep with the chickens," he said. "Mister, I'm sold out."

I brooded over my drink while he worked haphazardly behind the bar.

"Can you think of any place I might put up?" I said. "Somebody in town said maybe Mike Van Ness would have something."

He acquired an expression like that in the eyes of the county clerk when I had mentioned Mike Van Ness.

"Well—Mike's got a kind of a place," he said, "but I doubt if he's got any room now. See, the season started this morning and most everything is booked up."

"Maybe I could give Van Ness a call and find out," I said.

"Sure, if you want to."

I wonder what rubbed off on Mike Van Ness? I thought.

"I expect he's out hunting now though," Fingal said.

"Okay," I said, "do you mind if I walk around and have a look—see what I'm missing?"

"Help yourself," he said.

I walked over to the fireplace, where a fresh fire had been laid. The logs were big and comforting to look at. Sofas had been drawn up in front of the fireplace, and there were end tables and footstools. Thick, expensive and somewhat worn rugs were scattered over the hardwood floor. A nice room.

I wandered across to the other wall and scanned the photos. There were a lot of old stars—George Raft, Gary Cooper, Spencer Tracy. There were few women, but I saw a picture of Mae West, and Garbo was represented (some dreamer, I thought). Also Ed Fogel looked out at me, younger than he looked now, with an inscription to "Sam Fingal: Great White Hunter." And there was a publicity shot of Michele Armande, inscribed: "Love, darling Sam—Michele." She was very pretty with a slender, Gallic face, a real French pastry. I guessed the photo had been made at least fifteen years before.

"You've known a lot of celebrities," I said to Fingal.

"Oh yeah, plenty," he said. "Used to have some gay old times up here. Not so long ago either."

"You own the place?"

"Buying it," he said. "I bought it off Ed Fogel, the director, and some of his friends. Got a pretty good deal."

"I suppose it pays off," I said.

"Not like it used to."

I came to the end of my drink and set the glass on the bar. "Well," I said, "times change."

"Sure do. Want another?"

"No, thanks, I'd better get going—"

The telephone rang and I saw the woman in the office pick it up. I headed for the door, crossing the room diagonally. The woman in the office called to Sam:

"Sam! It's Chick—Chick Riordan. He wants—"

Sam Fingal's voice roared across the room. "Tell him to get lost!"

"Tell him yourself!" the woman yelled.

Sam Fingal came cursing behind me as I went on to the door, let myself out and headed for my car.

I got it started and turned around, drove a short distance, stopped on the deserted road and reached for the rifle on the back seat. I opened a box of ammo and loaded the gun and laid it on the floor of the front seat.

The game is getting edgy, I thought. Maybe I shouldn't have tried this on my own.

But Lieutenant Shapiro said he was tired.

155

14

I HAD to double back all the way to the North Pine cross-roads in order to get to the road that led to Mike Van Ness's place. I stopped at the gas station to fill the car and use the phone booth. I got Western Union and there was no message from Roy Rowley.

The station attendant was about twenty-three and friendly. "Looking for a place to stay?" he asked.

"Yeah—I see I'm a little late. Thought I might try Mike Van Ness."

"Oh," he said.

It might be an invitation—he had said it with a rising inflection.

"I don't know Mike Van Ness," I said, "—only the name."

"Uh, yeah. He used to be on the cops around here. Got in some trouble."

"Bad trouble?" I asked

"Bad enough to get kicked off the force. I don't know for sure what it was. He was on the vice squad, I heard, in Sacramento before he came over here."

"I didn't know they had vice in Sacramento," I said.

"Huh," he said, and that answered that.

I gave him my credit card and he processed it and gave me the receipt.

"Come to think of it," he said, "Mike probably got busted for busting some politician. You got to know who to leave alone."

I remembered—far back I remembered.

"True," I said, "true."

Back in the car, I asked, "I take this road to get to Van Ness's place?"

"Yeah, up there about three miles, past the cemetery, there's a mailbox, says Mike Van Ness on it. He don't run a regular place, but he's got some rooms he rents out. I don't know if he's got any now, being the season and all."

"I'll give it a try," I said.

"Good luck," he said.

It was an indigenous phrase in these parts.

I drove out of the station, put on the brakes, made a U-turn and drove into the station again.

"Forgot to make a phone call," I said.

The attendant nodded. "Help yourself," he said, waving to the booth.

He was working around nearby and I left the booth door open. I got the local operator and asked for long distance, Roy Rowley's number in Chicago. It took her a while to figure up the price. When she had it, I had to get some change from the attendant. To place the call I had to drop seven quarters and two dimes and I had half a dozen quarters to tide me over a couple of extra minutes.

Roy Rowley came on grumbling. "Listen," he said, "you know how many Patricia Whites there are?"

"Maybe a couple of thousand—"

157

"Would you believe ten? But I got it narrowed down to five hundred and eighty in California at the time you speak of."

"It was a long shot, but listen, I've got another one."

"Go ahead," he said.

"Mike Van Ness. Onetime vice cop in Sacramento, still living in vicinity of North Pine, California, once on local police, got busted. You got that?"

"Yeah," Roy said.

"I want to know when and why," I said.

"You could call our man in Sacramento, you know."

"I'd rather you would call him."

"If you say so."

"Reply to Western Union," I said, "I'm on the move."

"Okay, Mac."

I hung up and left the booth. The attendant hadn't moved far away, and he gave me a friendly wave as I left for the second time.

News, I trust, travels fast in a small town, I thought. Hopefully, not too fast—just fast enough.

I drove fairly fast west toward Mike Van Ness's place. Just before I reached his mailbox, I passed the Mountain View Memorial Park, a rural cemetery that appeared to be no longer in use. It had age over it like a cloud. It was badly tended, as far as I could see, and there was no gate to keep out marauders.

The mailbox was old and battered and the name Mike Van Ness was barely legible from the car. The road leading north was badly paved and I couldn't make much time over the chuckholes. The country was heavily wooded. At first I drove along the western edge of the cemetery; then the road veered off from it and I traveled two miles in thick woods before I came to Van Ness's rustic cabin in a cramped clearing. The place was about a third the size of North Pine Lodge, and I couldn't see from the outside where he could put up more than two and a half people besides himself.

The only car in sight was a dusty station wagon with a crushed left rear fender. I pulled up beside it, got out of the car and knocked on a door made of pine slabs. It bruised my knuckles and made very little sound. I looked for a bell but found none and pounded with my fist. The door rattled. After about a minute it opened and a guy looked out at me.

"Mike Van Ness?" I said.

His face was tight and deadpan. "Who's asking?" he said.

Still on the run, I thought. "Just a lonely hunter looking for a bed," I said.

He relaxed some. "Well, I tell you, it's pretty crowded around here. I've got a couple of guys and I don't have much space."

"I'll pay the prevailing rates," I said.

He looked back inside and said, "I've got a room—not much, but it's got a bed in it and a place to wash up. If you can make out in it—forty bucks."

"Forty a day?"

"That's the situation," he said.

"Could I take a look at it?"

"Sure."

He opened the door and stood back to let me in. I followed him across a small living room with Indian rugs on the floor, a fireplace and some odds and ends of furniture—chairs, tables, a sofa. There were no pictures on the

159

walls but there were a mounted moose head and a mounted fish. They could have been purchased from any number of taxidermists in the country.

Van Ness was as big as Sam Fingal, but younger, in good shape and not musclebound. I guessed his age to be not more than forty-one or forty-two. He wore boots and blue jeans and a tan sport shirt with a western yoke. His face was a good enough face, slightly scarred near the chin, but his nose was straight and his mouth was firm. He would appeal to girls, I decided. That always makes a good vice cop.

He opened a door in the corner of the room and showed me into a small chamber, hardly more than an alcove, containing a single bed, a dresser and a washstand on which were a big basin and a pitcher. There was a mirror of sorts over it. There was no rug on the floor, but the bed looked clean enough and there were blankets piled at the foot of it. There was one small window, high up over the bed.

"Like I said, it's not much," he said, "but you can have it if you want it."

"Forty bucks?"

"Yeah, well usually this season—but since you're getting a late start anyhow and there's only a few days to go—I'll let you have it for thirty-five."

"Okay," I said.

He seemed a little surprised, but he nodded and led me back to the living room where he opened a pad of receipts.

I thought up a name. "Arlo," I said. "Arlo McGovern."

He wrote laboriously. "How many nights?" he said.

"Well—say, two," I said.

He wrote some more, tore out the receipt and handed

it to me. I found a hundred-dollar bill in my wallet and showed it to him.

"I've got no change," he said.

"Well, take it and give me the change later."

"No. I got to go in town anyway and get change. I'll get straight with you when I come back."

"That's fine."

He put the receipt book away and got up. "You probably want to get out there," he said. "The others went out about daybreak. They won't be back till dark I guess. If I were you, I'd go down the north trail there to the creek and follow that for about a mile. There were ducks there yesterday and I got six nice ones early this morning."

"That's pretty good."

"Save enough ammo," he said, "so if you get lost you can start shooting."

"I'll try not to get lost," I said.

"It's been done."

He started away and turned back. "Probably play some poker tonight," he said. "The fellows out there now— and Sam Fingal usually comes over from North Pine. You play any?"

"Sure," I said.

"Good. I'll see you later then."

He went out by the front door. I sat and looked at the fireplace for a while, took a turn around the room, found a small, grubby kitchen with a big refrigerator and satisfied myself that there would be something to eat.

I stepped outside and Mike Van Ness was backing a car out of a large shed attached to one end of the cabin. The car was a new Porsche, polished and clean. He left it running and returned to close the shed door, but not before I caught sight of the vehicle that had been parked alongside the Porsche, a dusty panel truck, California license number NCA 487.

I started across to my own car as Van Ness pulled away, giving me a friendly wave as he went. I waved back, but I was less than lighthearted.

If those two are wandering around out there with guns, I thought, I had better get some extra troops.

I stuffed a couple of boxes of ammo in my pockets, lifted the gun from the floor and pulled the suitcase out of the back seat. Inside the cabin, I carried the suitcase to my room and put it on the bed. Carrying the gun, I checked out the cabin. There was a room next to mine with a double-decker bunk bed and some gear that appeared to belong to the other tenants. There were no name tags on it, but a Pan Am flight bag bore a sticker from the L. A. International Airport.

I wasn't interested in that stuff at the moment and left the room. A third bedroom, larger than either of the others, but still cramped and cluttered with belongings, opened off the corner opposite mine. It was disorderly but not unclean, and I took it to be Van Ness's room. There was an accumulation of old magazines and newspapers in one corner and a portable wardrobe stuffed with clothing, some outdoor, some dress. On the floor were a couple of pairs of boots and some street shoes. A high old-fashioned chiffonier stood in the middle of the wall opposite the bed. The upper drawers were filled with sox, underclothing and shirts and the bottom, and deepest, drawer was fitted with a padlock. That, naturally, was the one I wanted to explore.

The lock was a combination type of a fairly cheap

make. Most of those are pretty loose and I was sure I could crack it, but it might take a long time. Van Ness could be in town and back within half an hour without pushing too hard.

I blew on my hands and went to work, starting the turn to the right, as most of them start that way. It yielded a couple of times, but I overran the points and had to start over. After four tries I was fairly certain of the first three numbers and I worked very slowly, holding my breath half the time, looking for the final release. Twice I blew it and had to begin over again. The next time around I moved the dial one click at a time and I finally hit it, the thing opened.

The drawer was about half full. There was a stack of publicity photos similar to those on Sam Fingal's wall. Some were autographed, some were not. I saw no pertinent faces. Mixed in were half a dozen nudes, all but one of them standard stock photos. The exception was obviously a candid shot that had been blown up and it was pretty gamy. I didn't recognize the figure. There were a couple of bunches of letters wrapped with rubber bands and I found no names that meant anything to me. So far the contents were of the sort that any vice cop might accumulate in the course of a routine hitch. At the back of the drawer were some boxes of 8-mm. film in 100- and 200-foot rolls. I looked them over hurriedly. There were such identifying marks as Aggie-4, D-2, Ben-9, and those I could pretty well visualize without closer examination. But one box was labeled "Pat W. and M.," and that I wanted to see. I stuck it in my jacket pocket, looked through the rest and found nothing interesting. I restacked the boxes, arranged the contents as I had found them and got out of there.

I went to the car and put the box of film in the glove compartment. I knew I ought to get out on the hunting trail if I planned to continue the charade, but I hadn't had any sleep for a long time, and the way the clan seemed to be gathering, I didn't feel like sleeping on the premises.

I started the car, turned it and drove down the road to Mike Van Ness's mailbox. I hung there for a couple of minutes, then turned left, heading for the gas station at the North Pine corners. I needed a friend, I decided, and the attendant at the gas station was the closest possibility I could think of.

He wasn't any busier than he had been earlier and more than glad to do a servicing job on my car.

"I need a little sleep," I said. "Will it bother you if I take a nap on the back seat while you're working?"

That was a new one to him.

"Well—no," he said, "if you can sleep—"

"I can sleep anywhere I can put my head down."

It was no exaggeration. I got into the back seat and was asleep before he got the hoist in operation. I woke up a couple of times, once when he had to do some banging to loosen a wheel nut, and again when he lowered the hoist and moved the car to the battery cubicle. But I didn't lie awake long either time. When I woke for sure it was one thirty and I had had a good hour and fifteen minutes' nap. It made a good difference in my point of view. I paid the attendant and gave him a five-dollar tip. He was appreciative.

"You haven't got much hunting done, have you?" he said.

"No, I figured I'd get out early in the morning."

"Yeah. Look, if you're just nosing around for something easy, there's quail in the cemetery over there. I saw a flock of 'em yesterday. Hardly anybody ever goes in there and it seems like they know it's a safe place."

"Seems a shame to sneak up on them like that."

He looked doubtful. "I don't know," he said, "game is game."

"Right," I said. "I've got to go into town for a while. Maybe I'll try it when I get back."

"Okay," he said.

I drove into town and went to the Western Union office. There was a message from Roy Rowley and it read:

NOTHING ON P. WHITE FOR SURE. VAN NESS BUSTED FROM VICE SQUAD IN SACRAMENTO POLITICS AND BUSTED OFF COPS IN INYO COUNTY FOR BLACKMAIL ATTEMPT AGAINST UNIDENTIFIED MOVIE PERSONALITY. ANYTHING ELSE LET ME KNOW.

I folded the thing into my pocket and went out to the street. There was a camera shop a few doors down and I went in there and asked if I could rent the use of a projector for an hour or so.

"Hell," the proprietor said, "go ahead and use it. I got a screen in the back room."

He took me back there and set up a projector to hit a screen hung on the rear wall. I took the box of film from my pocket and fed it into the machine, while he hovered, ready to help me. When it was set to go I hesitated.

"Private film?" he said.

"In a way, yes," I said.

"I got it," he said. "I won't let anybody in."

165

He went out, closing the door, and I let it roll.

Nice friendly town, I was thinking, maybe a good place to settle down.

Then I quit thinking about that and watched the film.

It wasn't very well lighted and I could tell after a few feet that the camera was fixed—therefore probably hidden and the actors (and actresses) unaware that it was operating. I could tell by the way people kept moving in and out of range. The cast was quite interesting and, for the most part, familiar. There were Little Joe Caccelli and Ed Fogel and a big guy with a potbelly who looked like Sam Fingal. And as the picture progressed, there was Mike Van Ness. There were two girls and one of them resembled Michele Armande, though I had seen her—if I had seen her—only worn and dead, except for the photo on Sam Fingal's wall. The other girl was a stranger. She was a faded blonde, older than Michele.

Neither of the girls had any clothes on, and Ed Fogel was stripped to the waist. Joe Caccelli was fully dressed and Van Ness and Fingal were in shirtsleeves. The girls bore the brunt of the action and they were obviously far gone on booze. The blonde especially kept falling down at unlikely junctures, but Michele was also loaded beyond the power of right reason.

It was an orgiastic scene in which nothing very unusual happened—in the context of orgies—until quite suddenly, without apparent cause, the two girls got into a fight. It looked like a real one right from the start. Blood appeared. At first the males cheered them on, but as the battle got more ferocious, guys stepped in to break it up. Again suddenly a man's naked arm and hand swung, striking the blonde in the face. I couldn't tell for sure

166

about the force of the blow, but she fell all right and her head hit the corner of a table. She rolled over once and lay still. Michele, off balance, fell toward her but rolled away and half sat up, looking dazed. Then Little Joe Caccelli was in the scene making authoritative gestures and that was all there was. The camera had evidently run out of film.

I turned off the light, rewound the thing and got it into the box and into my pocket. Somebody knocked. I said, "Come in," and the proprietor stuck his head in.

"Sorry, I got to get a—"

"It's all right, come on in," I said.

I went out to the front of the shop. There were a couple of customers and I waited around while the proprietor took care of them and got free. When we were alone I asked him, "Do you have some processed movie film I could buy?"

He looked wary.

"Well, I got some eight-millimeter stuff, scenic stuff, ride around Lake Tahoe, stuff like that."

"That's fine," I said.

"Fifty, hundred, hundred and fifty—" he said.

"A hundred," I said.

"What kind of scenes did you want? You want to see the list?"

"No, I don't care what scene it is."

He shrugged, picked a box off the shelf and handed it to me.

"Grand Canyon," he said. "Very pretty."

"That will do," I said.

It cost five-forty. I gave him the money, thanked him for the use of the machine and got back to the car. I drove out of town, stopped, switched the two films, putting the scenic item in Mike Van Ness's box, then locked the death film in the trunk of the car. I put the other in my jacket pocket. Then I drove back to the North Pine corners, turned right and drove to the cemetery.

15

I LEFT the car in a grove of trees near the cemetery gate and took my rifle with me. It was only about three thirty and the air was comfortable, but the sun had disappeared beyond the western mountains and it was gloomy and like day's end in the woods. The grass in the cemetery was overgrown and there was no sign of recent traffic. I glanced at headstones as I walked and found most of them to be dated long before, some as many as fifty years. Now and then a more recent date would show, but the most recent I could find at first was of about twelve years before. The older headstones were quite large and handsome and the stonecutter had done an ornate job. The later ones were smaller and simpler. Some were simply flat to the ground with brass plates bolted to them. After a while I made out a pattern in the plots. Family grounds were grouped down a center area from the entrance stretching back as far as the park extended. On either side were single graves, many with markers so modest they suggested a pauper's field.

I moved off to the right, scanning the names as I passed above them. Elmer Cassidy, 1893–1957; Elizabeth Mears,

169

1924–1948; Chauncey Fitzgerald, 1877–1932, and on and on, one after another. It grew darker. I rounded the last row of markers and crossed to the other side. By this time I had to bend down and look closely in order to read the names. I read twelve before I found the grave of Michele Armande, 1926–1960. It was a small, plain marker and obviously had had no more attention than any of the others in recent times.

A high-pitched yelping sound came from somewhere off to my left, a dog sound. Trees and ground cover were thick in that direction and I couldn't find a path through them. I decided not to bother with it and then the yelping sounded again, lower pitched, but urgent. I pushed my way through the undergrowth and came into a clearing. The cemetery fence was broken down at the corner, and beyond I could see the marks of a makeshift road, no more than a lane leading away westward. Not far from the fence, what looked like a dog was pawing at the ground.

I moved a few feet nearer, stopped and checked the load in my rifle. It was no dog, more likely a wolf, wild and scrawny-looking. And then I reminded myself of where I was and realized it was neither dog nor wolf, but a coyote. I was surprised to see it alone. They travel in packs.

The wind was on my side and he let me get to within thirty feet of him, then he looked up and growled. I stood still. He sniffed the air, started away, then returned, hungry and intent, to paw some more. I made out a longish mound of earth, freshly turned. The animal was digging at it with determination now. A chipmunk skittered out from under a bush and the coyote snapped at it as it passed, then went back to his digging. He had a hole started but he wasn't down very far. The mound was about six feet long and of ragged dimensions.

I moved closer and the coyote bared his teeth at me, very ugly, hunched over his find.

"Brother," I said, startled at the sound of my own voice, "I hate to do this, but it looks like you or me, and I've got the gun."

I moved two steps closer and he crouched very low, hugging the mound, growling at me with those bad teeth showing. I lifted the gun and sighted and squeezed off. It was a clean hit. He keeled over without a sound. I went over there and studied him a minute and he was finished all right. I used the gun muzzle to push him clear of the mound of dirt, and then I did some digging of my own, using the stock of the rifle.

It didn't take long. I got deep enough to run into a different kind of resistance. Then, reluctantly, I used my hands to clear dirt away from the dead face of the woman I had been told was Michele Armande. It was less horrifying than I would have expected. She looked peaceful and at home, the way the dead should look.

I pushed dirt back over her, glanced at the dead coyote and thought about it. If the pack shows up, I thought, they'll do away with her. But maybe, with luck, they'll do away with their own dead in preference to digging. Or maybe he was an old loner and the pack is through with him. I would have to take the chance.

It was nearly dark as I moved back through the graveyard to where I had left the car. I went on the double the last thirty yards and was winded when I got under the wheel.

I drove to the gas station at North Pine and the attendant was cleaning up.

"Hi," he said. "Heard a shot up in the graveyard. That you?"

"Yeah, I missed," I said. "Are you about to close?"

"Pretty soon. Isn't much business after six."

"Do you know anybody who'd like to earn a hundred bucks for about twelve hours' easy work?"

For the first time, his friendliness turned to caution. "To do what?" he said.

"Drive a car—this car—to Los Angeles and return by air."

"Oh . . . well, I got a day off tomorrow . . ."

"And you're free from the time you close here?"

"I can close early," he said.

"Where do you normally go from here?"

"Up in town. I live in town."

"Uh . . . ," I said.

"But I don't have to get home any special time."

"Could you hang around here for a while, as long, maybe, as three, four hours?"

"For a hundred, sure."

"Could you close it up right now long enough to drive me back to Mike Van Ness's place then bring the car back here?"

"Sure, why not?"

It took him a couple of minutes to lock the pumps and the door of the office. I let him drive and he did all right with it. We didn't make any conversation till we were on the private road leading to Van Ness's cabin. Then he said, "Mister, you some kind of a cop?"

"Yes," I said. "Is that all right with you?"

"Sure thing," he said. "As long as you've got a hundred dollars."

I got out my wallet, opened it, showed him two bills and he nodded.

"Sure thing," he said.

"I'm not sure how things will go," I said. "If I don't show up in four hours, will you call the nearest sheriff's station and tell them to get over to Mike Van Ness's place? And if I turn up before that, be ready to leave on very short notice."

"I got it," he said.

"You can let me out here," I said.

He stopped the car and let me out. I reached in the glove compartment and took out the roll of film in the box marked "Pat W.—" and stuck it in my pocket.

"I'll be there," he said. "Just say when."

"Right," I said. "Thanks for the ride."

He grinned and waved and started backing down the road to a place where he could turn around.

It was dark on the road, but there was light enough to get me across the clearing to Mike Van Ness's cabin. There was a light burning inside. As I approached, two guys in hunting costume came out, heading for the station wagon. They were strangers and we waved in passing.

I knocked on the door and Mike Van Ness opened it. I went in, carrying the rifle, and he said, "Any luck?"

"Nope," I said. "I guess I don't know where to look."

He didn't say anything. I went on to my room, went inside and laid the rifle on the bed. When I came out, Van Ness was standing near the kitchen door with a can of beer in one hand and a shotgun in the other.

"You walked a lot, huh?" he said.

"Quite a lot. I left my car at the gas station to be serviced. First thing in the morning, the guy said."

He drank some of the beer.

"Any way I can buy a drink?" I said.

"Help yourself," he said.

He was very tight. I knew something had crashed, but I couldn't tell how much noise it had made.

He nodded toward the kitchen and I went in there, found some ice in a bowl and a bottle of whiskey and made myself a light drink.

"The poker game still on?" I said.

"No. Those two decided not to play. They went into town, to a show."

"Oh, I was looking forward to it," I said.

"Uh-huh."

He drained his beer and turned into the kitchen. I heard him open the refrigerator and take out another can. I sat down on the sofa facing the fireplace, and when he came in again he had a fresh can of beer.

"Maybe Riordan and Dennis would like a game," I said. "Of poker, I mean."

The shotgun muzzle wiggled.

"What do you want?" he said.

"Nothing much," I said.

"You been nosing around all over, courthouse—you got a tracer on me. What do you want?"

"Some information," I said.

"You're a private eye, huh?"

"That's right."

"What kind of information?"

"Which of the men was it who knocked Patricia White

down so that she cracked her head against the table and
died—at North Pine Lodge about eight years ago?"

The shotgun stiffened in his hand. "It wasn't me," he
said.

"All right, who was it?"

"I don't know."

"Let's try another one. Whose idea was it to make it
look like Michele Armande?"

He hesitated.

"Little Joe Caccelli?" I said.

"I don't know," he said.

"You were there."

"You tell me I was there."

"I've got the film," I said.

He just looked at me.

"I got it out of the bottom drawer of your dresser in
your bedroom."

He held the gun steady. He could hit me all right
from where he was. He wouldn't have to aim much.

"You're talking yourself into a grave," he said.

"Maybe," I said, "but I've got the film. Not on me,
though. It's in a safe place, with directions where it should
be sent if anything happens to me. Along with a full report."

"A full report on what?"

"Come on," I said. "Let's get it together. You help me
and I will help you."

He didn't want to believe me, but he almost had to.
Even if he hadn't killed Pat White himself, he had certainly been in on the conspiracy to frame Michele.

"What do you want?" he said.

"Two things. All the information I can get, and the

corpse of Michele Armande that is buried over there on the edge of the cemetery."

"And what do I get?"

"The film."

"Where is it?"

"It's in a safe place."

"When do I get it?"

"After we get the corpse of Michele Armande loaded into the panel truck in your shed."

"What about Riordan and Dennis?"

"That's up to you. I've got nothing against them."

He drank some beer, watching me over the top of the can.

"You're pretty cool, huh?" he said.

I shrugged and had some of my own drink. It was far too weak to sustain me. I wasn't cool at all but I managed not to shake.

He threw his beer can into the fireplace and hunkered down, the shotgun across his knees aimed casually in my direction.

"Listen, I didn't have anything to do with it," he said. "I got a call and I went over there to the lodge—"

"When did you get the call? On the film, you're cavorting around with the rest of them."

"I got a call earlier, from Michele. She was worried about the way things were going."

"All right."

"So I got over there and they were having a party, and I didn't want to give Michele away, so I just joined the thing. That's why I did that."

"Well, so what happened?"

"Things got pretty wild—if you saw the film—and the girls got in a fight. A couple of us tried to break it up, and then somebody, I don't know who it was, gave Patty a belt and she dropped."

"Everybody was pretty drunk?"

"Yeah—I wasn't drunk, but everybody else was."

"You did have presence of mind enough to save the film."

"I took the film for evidence."

"Ever turn it in?"

"Would you?" he said.

"I don't know. I think so."

"Anyway—this guy Caccelli took charge."

"What was in it for Caccelli?"

"He had some kind of deal with Fogel, the director, and it was a bad scene for Fogel, bad publicity, and Caccelli figured a way to cool everything."

He was talking freely now. I could put it down partly to relief at getting it off his chest. But also, he wanted that film and he didn't want to have to kill me for it.

"Caccelli persuaded Michele that she had killed Patty White, is that the way it went?"

"Yeah. It wasn't too hard. She was out of her skull."

"And this Patty White—who was she?"

"Nobody, a nothing. That's how it could work. She came from nowhere, nobody knew her, no family, no friends, nothing. She could disappear."

"Or Michele could become Patty White."

"Well . . . yeah, I guess that's what they did."

"And you went along with all this?"

"Sure, why not?"

I looked at him and shrugged. "I don't know why not, if you don't," I said.

"What's your thing in this? What do you want with Michele's body?"

"I want to get it back in the proper jurisdiction," I said, "to save my face."

"You know who killed her?"

"I think so, but that's not your problem."

He fingered the trigger of the gun. It had to be a nervous gesture, but I wished he wouldn't.

"Let's get that corpse," I said.

He got up readily enough. I managed to get out of the direct line of fire in case the gun should go off. He didn't bother to make an adjustment.

"You have the key to the truck?" I asked.

"Key's in it," he said.

"Can we get to the grave by a back road?"

"Yeah."

"Then let's get it done."

After a short hesitation I went ahead of him. It was improbable that he would blast me at this point. There was the uncertainty about that film. But an improbability is a thin comfort when you're walking away from the open end of a shotgun.

I fumbled some at the door, but got it open and went outside. There was only the light from the cabin, but as I passed out of it, heading for the shed, a searchlight beam flashed on behind me. Van Ness would have picked it up on his way out.

There was no lock on the shed, but a peg stuck into the hasp. I pulled it out and pushed the door back and the truck was standing where I had last seen it. Leaning against the wall was a shovel. I opened the back of the truck, threw the shovel in and looked around for Van Ness. A guy shouted. Van Ness was in the open doorway, probing the yard with the light beam. Riordan and Dennis came at a trot toward the shed.

178

"Hold it!" Van Ness said.

They stopped, then separated suddenly and Riordan pulled a pistol out of his pocket and leveled it. The blast of Van Ness's shotgun rocked the shed. It was a heavy load at short range and Riordan sprawled backward.

Goddam! I thought.

"Dennis," Van Ness said, "come over here."

Dennis came on, walking slowly, cursing Van Ness.

"You crummy sell-out—"

"Shut up," Van Ness said.

"Okay," I said, "it was self-defense. Let's get going."

"Get in the back of the truck, Dennis," Van Ness said.

After a second, Dennis unlatched the door and climbed in beside the shovel.

"You drive," Van Ness said to me.

I swung up under the wheel. Van Ness got around the truck and climbed in beside me. He knocked the glass out of the rear window above the seat and poked the muzzle through it.

"Just ride along, Dennis," he said.

Dennis swore at him some more.

"Shut up, dum-dum," Van Ness said. "You should have known better than to come back up here."

Dennis shut up. I got the lights on, backed out of the shed and asked Van Ness which way to go.

"Around the end of the shed," he said, "you'll pick up the tracks to your right."

There was a lot of high grass back there, but when the light beams hit it I could make out a recent car-track winding among the trees.

"Go ahead," Van Ness said, "it's firm enough."

It was firm all right, but it was bumpy as hell. Van Ness watched over Dennis in the back as I pushed through the hard ruts. I was beginning to wish we had taken the long way around when I saw the broken fence at the corner of the cemetery. I got up close to it, turned the truck around and backed it into the cemetery as far as I dared. When I stopped we were within about twenty-five feet of Michele's shallow grave.

Van Ness opened the truck door and told Dennis to get out and bring the shovel. Dennis grumbled and Van Ness wiggled the gun at him. With the example of Riordan fresh in his memory, Dennis made his decision and came along, carrying the shovel.

The coyote was lying where I had left him. Dennis snarled and pitched the carcass away with the shovel.

"Okay," Van Ness said, "get her up out of there."

Van Ness held the light and Dennis started digging. I stood around, trying to figure out why everybody was being so helpful. It finally came through to me that Van Ness looked on me as someone like himself. He could trust me, because, like him, I was corruptible.

Dennis uncovered the corpse in about fifteen minutes. They had wrapped her in a blanket, but it had come away from her face. I wished it hadn't.

"Let's get her in the truck," I said.

I went to the feet and left the head and shoulders to Dennis. When I lifted, the body tilted like a board.

After all, I thought, she's only been dead about forty-eight hours, and the cold would slow down the process.

Her feet were ridiculously small in my hands. Dennis lifted with me and we carried her to the truck and laid her on the floor. Most of the dirt from the grave had spilled off her.

I headed for the front seat and Van Ness said, "Just a minute."

I looked around at him. He had the gun under his arm and the light in his other hand.

"The film," he said.

I had forgotten about it.

"Back at the cabin," I said.

He stared at me.

"You son of a bitch," he said.

"Yeah," I said.

He made Dennis get in the back with the corpse and he got in front with me.

I drove back over the rough ground to the shed, rounded it, leaving the truck pointed toward the road, and stopped. Van Ness watched me closely as I got out. I felt the truck lurch in the back, but Van Ness was intent on the film. He slid across the seat to follow me out and I backed off, waiting. Dennis came from the back of the truck and jumped Van Ness from behind. I jumped and hit the ground when the gun went off. When I looked up, Dennis and Van Ness were rolling over and over on the ground, clawing at each other. The gun was lying a few feet away. I picked it up and got on my feet.

"Break it up," I said.

Then I recalled that Van Ness had fired both barrels and the gun wasn't any use to anybody without reloading. I threw it on the ground as Van Ness and Dennis came up, snarling at each other. I got in the truck, started the engine and got it rolling. Van Ness turned toward it and I tossed the box of film at him.

"Good-bye," I said, "and good luck."

I got the truck onto the road and opened it up, heading for the North Pine crossroads. It wouldn't take Van Ness long to find out I had pulled a switch on him.

The station was dark, but my car was parked on the

open end of the drive and my guy was sitting in it smoking a cigaret. I drove the truck up beside him, left it running and talked to him through the car window. I gave him the Redgrave Avenue address and made him repeat it three or four times.

"You'll remember?" I said.

"I got a good memory," he said.

"Wait there for me. You'll probably get there first. Don't try to keep me in sight, just get down there to L.A."

"Sure thing," he said.

I got back in the truck. I had a head start, but he passed me up within half a mile and I never saw him again till we met on Redgrave Avenue.

16

It was still dark when I pulled off the freeway in West Los Angeles and called Lieutenant Shapiro. He wasn't in and I left a message with his sergeant.

"Here's what to do," I said. "Pick up Joe Caccelli on the complaint I told the Lieutenant I would sign. Pick up Ed Fogel the movie director on a charge of conspiracy in kidnapping—Caccelli's charge. Bring them both to twenty-six-oh-five Redgrave Avenue in Culver City, to identify the body of Michele Armande. Better start now."

"I'll call the Lieutenant," he said.

I got back on the freeway and drove to Culver City. Not till then did I give much thought to the load I was carrying. The sweat broke out all over me at once. I slowed to forty-five miles an hour and hugged the right side of the road. I tried to think of what a highway patrolman would say if he stopped me on a traffic thing, took a look in the back of the truck and found Michele Armande. But I didn't like thinking about what he would say and I shut it out of my mind. As it happened I made it to Redgrave Avenue without incident. My loyal gas station attendant was sitting in my car, parked on the street, smoking a cigaret.

I paused beside the car and said, "I've got to go around the back. You can help me, if you agree to, but you don't have to."

He was feeling pretty good.

"Sure thing," he said.

He left the car and got in beside me. I remembered the film in the car trunk, got out and found it and put it in the pocket of the hunting jacket I was still wearing. Then we drove around to the alley and stopped at Michele Armande's back door. Out of natural curiosity, the boy took a look into the back of the truck. His eyes went a little wider than usual, but that was all the reaction he showed. He was a good man.

"I've got to get that body into the house," I said. "If you don't want to—"

"Hell, let's get it done," he said.

"The door is locked," I said, "and I'll have to bust in."

"Okay," he said.

It had begun to get light and there would be traffic in and out of the alley any minute. The apartment door was so loose in the frame I could almost—but not quite —open it with my hands. I sent the kid for the shovel and showed him how to get it into the opening and pry the thing loose from the lock. With all that leverage, it was no great trick, but when the door sprung, he dropped the shovel and it made a hell of a noise on the pavement. A woman stuck her head out a back window.

"Who's there?" she said. "I'll call the police!"

"Ma'am, I wish you would," I said. "I'm expecting them any minute."

She slammed the window down. The kid helped me

pull the corpse out of the truck and we got her inside and around the corner and into the bedroom. I looked through the closet, found a silk scarf, got it around her neck and hung her from the bedpost. The kid walked away, dusting his hands together, knocking off loose grave dirt.

"I been thinking about joining the cops myself," he said.

"Think it over hard," I said.

There was loud knocking at the front door. I found the light switch in the front room and opened up for Shapiro, his sergeant, a couple of other cops, and Little Joe Caccelli, who was hotter than a gasoline fire.

"If you don't let me call my lawyer," he was saying, "I'll have the whole goddamned L.A. police force—"

"Yeah, Caccelli," Shapiro said. And to me he said, "Where is it?"

"Right this way," I said.

I walked them back to the bedroom and stood aside to let Shapiro, Caccelli and the sergeant go in. I waited in the hall. I had seen enough of Michele Armande. The kid from North Pine was sitting on a sofa in the living room, smoking a cigaret.

"Where's Fogel?" I asked one of the cops.

"We can't locate him yet."

In the bedroom, Shapiro was saying, "Is that Michele Armande?"

"I wouldn't tell you your own goddamned name—" Caccelli said.

I looked in there.

"I've got the film, Caccelli," I said. "I got it off Mike Van Ness at North Pine. You're on it, along with Fogel and Van Ness and Sam Fingal and Patricia White. You want me to run it for you?"

Caccelli wouldn't look at me.

"I say nothing," he said. "Nothing."

Shapiro looked at me. "You have a complaint to make against Joseph Caccelli?" he said.

"Yes, sir," I said. "He kidnapped me."

"Caccelli?" Shapiro said.

"I say nothing."

"All right," Shapiro said to his sergeant. "Take him downtown and book him."

"I want to call my lawyer!" Caccelli roared.

"You can call him from downtown," the sergeant said.

The other cops stepped into it and they took Caccelli out of the room. I went with Shapiro into the living room and introduced him to the kid from North Pine.

"He was a big help to me," I said. "He's thinking about joining the cops."

"Good for him," Shapiro said. "Tell me about things."

My arm started to ache badly. I sat down on the sofa and took a couple of breaths.

"You'll have to see the film to get into it," I said.

I told him about what happened during the wild party, according to the film, and the corroboration I'd gotten from Mike Van Ness.

"Who was it struck the White girl?" Shapiro asked.

"Fogel," I said. "It was a naked arm that hit her. Fogel was the only guy there without a shirt at the time."

"So then Caccelli stepped in?"

"To protect Fogel mostly. Michele was out of her mind with booze and fright and they convinced her she had killed Pat White. They rigged the scheme to bury the White girl as Michele, and Michele took on Pat White's identity. It wasn't too bad a plan—the White girl had no identity anyway and it was unlikely anyone would ever

186

come looking for her. The main weakness was that in time Michele's memory would clear and she would realize that she had been badly bamboozled. This eventually came to pass and she got fed up with living in anonymous squalor and wanted out. The first one she put the arm on, naturally, was Fogel."

"Why?" Shapiro asked.

"They had been playmates once. Michele had plenty on Fogel, including murder. It looked like Rinaldi at first —because they were legally married and all. But Rinaldi had married her to keep her in this country, and as a convenience to Fogel, to whom Rinaldi was obligated. Rinaldi didn't tell me all this, though he told me some of it. Both he and Caccelli wanted to protect Fogel, because they had a stake in him—Caccelli had money and his wife's career in it, and Rinaldi had the emotional obligation to protect Abigail, Mary Dane's daughter. Anyway, it has to be Fogel that Michele would put the heat on because he was the one who had the most power—and money.

"He could put her off as long as she played at being Patricia White. But when she got desperate enough to abandon the role and become Michele Armande again, he had to do something. It was only in the last few days, I think, she changed her identity again. That was too much and Fogel killed her.

"Caccelli had to step in again and he got a little too wild this time, and that business of stealing the corpse and all was a lot of hysterical nonsense. Then he tried to make it look like Rinaldi—he did better with that, because of the background, trying to get Rinaldi to take Michele under his wing—but Caccelli's lieutenants are clumsy."

"Where and how did Fogel kill Michele?"

187

"I don't know, you'll have to ask him. Not here, I think, though maybe. I think he did it in a rage and then panicked and called Caccelli, and Caccelli started rigging the hanging and all that."

"You don't have any hard evidence—physical?"

"No, not really. But you let Fogel watch that film a few minutes, and he'll crack. I'll give you twenty to one on it."

"Where's the film?"

"Oh, I forgot—here."

I took it out of my pocket and gave it to him.

"Says scenic tour of the Grand Canyon," he said

"Yeah, I know. But have a look at it."

I got up.

"I've got some more questions," Shapiro said.

"I know. I've got some more answers too, but first I got to go home and take a bath. That panel truck out back belongs to Caccelli, I guess. You know what to do with it."

"Sure."

"Come on," I said to the kid from North Pine, "You probably want to freshen up too."

"You'll be in your office? Shapiro said.

"Right."

I nearly fell down getting into the car and the kid offered to drive. I let him. I was sound asleep when we got to the office, and he had to wake me up. Inside, he stretched out on the couch and I got in the bathtub and fell asleep again.

At about eight thirty in the morning I was lying on the couch in my dressing gown and slippers when the door opened and Gilda came dancing in.

188

"Where have you been?" she said. "I've been trying to call you. You know what your horoscope reads like for today?"

"Groove, baby," I said. "Impart the news to me."

"It's very serious. It says you should avoid all questionable contacts and rely solely on your own judgment in every undertaking and preferably you should not leave the house."

I caught her hand and pulled her down on the couch.

"I never read a horoscope that pleased me more," I said. "Bless you."

The kid from North Pine came out of the bedroom. Gilda pulled free and got up. I introduced them. His name was Paul—Paul Smith.

"That's a good name," Gilda said. "When were you born?"

The kid stared at her.

"Go ahead, tell her," I said. "You'll never regret it."

"Sure enough," he said. "August—August twenty-first."

"Let's see," Gilda said, "just a minute, I'll be right back."

She skipped away.

"She's all right in the head?" Paul said.

"She's fine in the head."

I gave him his hundred dollars and enough money to get to the airport and to buy a ticket home. He would have to fly to Sacramento and take a bus to North Pine. He didn't mind. I invited him to stay and have some breakfast, but he guessed he'd better get back. He could get in some hunting later in the day, and the next day he would have to work. As soon as he was gone, I fell asleep.

189

Gilda was sitting at my desk, watching me sleep, when Shapiro finally called at about noon. She brought the phone to me.

"Fogel cracked," Shapiro said. "We ran the film for him and Caccelli, and they started laying it on each other and Fogel cracked wide open."

"I had a hunch," I said.

"You must have had more." he said.

"Well . . . tell you something about Fogel, he tends to panic and do himself in. He came to see me the night I found Michele—the first time, I mean—and he said something about a murder. So I said somebody must have talked to him and he vigorously denied it. But he had no reason to deny it. Later Rinaldi told me he had called Fogel and told him about it. A guy who can lose his head that easy is a guy who can kill, and then yell for help.

"I knew there was something working between Fogel and Caccelli. When Caccelli and his freak were setting me up for the ride, Fogel came in unexpectedly and made a few aimless remarks and then went away. Caccelli let him go. So Caccelli had something on Fogel, who pretended to be concerned about what they were doing to me. But he was clumsy about it and it didn't make any sense."

"All right, but I wish I had something more . . . physical."

"Just keep the pressure on Fogel. He'll find the evidence for you if he has to create it himself. He can't stay on his own side for thirty seconds at a time."

"Okay, Mac."

"Anyway—that corpse was real, huh?" I said.

"Yes," Shapiro said, "it was real."

"Excuse me now, I got to call Mary Dane and tell her everything is all right."

"So long," Shapiro said, "I'll drop around."

He hung up. I looked at Gilda, who was pouting.

"Who's Mary Dane?" she said.

"A friend of mine," I said, "and of Peter Rinaldi's. Maybe we can go visit her one of these days. She's a great movie star."

"I'd like that," she said.

"We'll do it."

The sun was hot and bright in the windows and I got up and drew the curtains.

We never did go to visit Mary Dane. We put it off, the way you put things off, and she died before we got around to it. Peter Rinaldi moved to the MPRF retirement home, and I never saw him again either. S.

Dewey, J.
The Taurus
trip

196